Invasion Book 2: D

By

J.F. Holmes

Prologue

Alien invasions were the thing of Science Fiction. Impossible! Never happen! No reason! Interstellar flight, impossible, takes too long. Anyone that advanced would have no need. Why would they bother?

And yet … the first Invy scoutship hammered the old International Space Station to a cloud of debris with a rail gun round. Why? Because they could. A very human reaction, if you think about it. And the small piece of the station, the next orbit, that blew a hole through the scout's hull and dropped it down in a cornfield in Nebraska, the autopilot delivering the dead crew right into our hands? Stupid luck, we thought, and now we have a chance. The NSA took six months to crack the encryption on their computers. It was another two months before linguists, with the help of our first Sentient AI's, understood their language. It took another month, a limited nuclear war in the South China Sea, the death of thousands of soldiers and civilians, and a kinetic strike on Kennedy Space Center from another scout ship, to unite the world in facing the threat. We had some time. Time that saw a massive focus of energy and capital.

For a year and a half, we built. Reverse engineered Invy technology, what we could grasp of it. They were ahead of us, yes, but not too far ahead, which makes sense. Otherwise, we would be done. Antimatter reactors, small enough to power capital class ships. Rail guns the US Navy had been developing fitted onto hulls named after old battleships. *Potemkin, Iowa, Victory, Yamato*, and a dozen more, each group representing the pride of their countries. Carriers, *Lexington, Hiru, Ark Royal* and others formed the core of the fleets, squadrons of fighters hastily thrown together and staffed with the best pilots of each nation. Into each of the capital ships was installed the incredibly complex and expensive Artificial Intelligences, the first children of Man, put to our most ancient practice, war. The best and brightest of our young men and women were selected for command, trained under intense pressure, fought their way through a thousand simulations, and emerged victorious. Experimental neural links, surgically implanted, were put into these teenaged commanders, giving them instant access to terabytes of data, and they helmed the ships, ran the war.

There were those, though, who asked, "What if we lose? What then?" They were ignored, for the most part. They were mainly veterans of older wars, ones who had fought tenacious enemies who had never been defeated, despite overwhelming superior firepower. What if it was our turn to be crushed? What then?

Some listened. The ground forces, deemed useless, had been put aside in favor of the glorious new space navy, so the Confederated Earth Forces army started digging. They begged, borrowed, and stole whatever funds they could. Mothballed Cold War bunkers were reactivated. Tanks, Armored Personnel Carriers, Helicopters, Planes, all deemed useless, were wrapped in preservative and put into climate controlled caverns. Old manuals about insurgency were dusted off. Contingency plans were laid, often without the political arm of the government aware. Special Forces teams focused on being able to train populations in survival and rebellion. Scout Teams relearned the art of gathering intelligence without the reliance on modern technology. Citizens with critical skills were identified to be kept safe in a crisis.

All this went on quietly. When anyone asked, the US Secretary of Defense, prime mover behind Operation Moria, just answered, "So what? If we win, we win. If we lose, well, what will you care? You'll be dead."

And we lost. The fleet was smashed, easily. Just as a PT boat could give little indication of the capabilities of an Aircraft Carrier, the Invy Scout ship had been a bare bones affair, and we hadn't learned a tenth of what the Invy could do. The alien's magnetic shielding shrugged off our rail guns, and automated defenses stripped our fighters from the sky. Yes, we hurt them, but in the end, we traded three dozen of the most expensive constructions known to man for just two of the Invaders' smaller ships. The seventeen year old commander of the Confederated Earth Forces Navy, General David Warren, was arrested and made a scapegoat for the politicians who had insisted on continuing a losing battle, of throwing away the fleet.

What followed was a month of panic, and then the orbital bombardment began. Power plants. Road junctions. Rail routes. Airports. Canals. Communication facilities. Military bases. Every ship at sea bigger than twenty meters. The Invaders held the high ground, and they methodically destroyed everything that made for a modern civilization. The only landing they made was to capture the CEF Headquarters at Cheyenne Mountain. A two day pitched battle there saw most of the remaining US military destroyed, struck down by rods from space, even as they fought the Invy troops to a standstill. Their tech was only just better than ours, and we were fighting for our survival, but whomever held the high ground won.

Then they watched us starve, fight each other, and descend into barbarism, for two years. At the end of that, the invaders released a spread of Nano particles that were programed to attack the small bit of DNA that differentiated humans from their closest relatives. From thirty degrees south to thirty degrees north, for the ruling Dragons preferred the tropics for their cities, every human being died a horrible, bloody death. The tropics because a no-go zone for humanity.

Through it all, the men and women of the Confederated Earth Forces waited, and watched as their world fell, in their underground bunkers. Helplessly, because their families were outside. They waited, and watched, and when, the year after the plague, the Invaders spread out to establish towns, which were in reality slave pens for the remains of humanity, they acted. The Invy, no stranger to swaying masses, cloaked their occupation in terms of environmentalism, saving the Earth from overpopulation and pollution. It was manipulation to keep the population sedate, and, after the hunger years, many responded.

The Invy, to control Earth's population, prevent travel in groups more than three. Individual farms are allowed, but the only towns are limited to five thousand people, and are controlled by the Invy. All people in the towns and outlying areas are registered by facial recognition, and attackers were quickly identified and their homes destroyed. Space stations dropped titanium rods on any radio sources or identified attack locations, with the force of a small nuclear bomb.

Small teams moved out, blended into the population, and worked to impede the reeducation of humanity. Targeted assassination of collaborators. Selective sabotage. Literature to counter the Invy's seeming hopeful message of repair to the environment, to explain the reality of their slavery. Identifying those who still had some fight left.

In the destroyed cities, groups of men and women trained, hiding in the ruins, forming individual platoons that could, someday, operate the equipment hidden in mine shafts, old rail tunnels, and natural caverns in the ground. Called Main Force units, they came from the farms and homesteads outside the Invy towns, moved only in pairs, and tried to preserve the spirit of the fight.

At sea, the submarines hid below the surface, avoiding the eyes in the sky, keeping their precious nuclear weapons pristine and ready to strike, while planners tried to come up with a way to win. Engineers worked on captured equipment, looking for ways to counteract higher levels of tech.

The Scouts moved out, also. To watch. To listen. To learn. To know their enemy so well that, when the day came, they could strike back, hard. To strike back and win. Reduced to nineteenth century technology, they walked, and moved from Invy town to occupation base to hidden bunker, gathering knowledge.

Then the day came, the word was given, and the war began. Operation Red Dawn was a last chance strike to liberate Earth. In a series of coordinated actions, CEF troops, aircraft and ships attacked to neutralize the Invy control of the high ground, and seize important bases. In the Western Pacific Ocean, submarines launched the remaining modified surface to orbit missiles to knock out one station, while fighters from Japan provided air cover against attacking Invy craft. In the Atlantic, heavy lasers attempted to blind another orbital, to give attacking ground forces a chance. The Scout Teams' mission, in America, England and Japan, was to seize Invy shuttle craft, load them with assault troops, and capture the orbitals. Main force armor and infantry conducted attacks to capture regional bases and neutralize Invy ground power.

In space, General David Warren, once teenaged leader of the CEF forces, who had been in hiding for more than a decade, resumed command. In contact with the surviving Artificial Intelligences, together human and AI waged war on the nets and against Invy cruisers with the surviving carrier, *U.S.S. Lexington.*

This is the story of that day.

Backdrop, the setting of Day of Battle.

Invasion: Day of Battle is a series of six stories that tell of actions on the first day of the war against the occupiers of Earth, the Invaders, or "Invy". Several of the stories are continuations of stories from *Invasion: Resistance*, but all can be read as individual pieces. Together, they form a narrative of the combat from the first twenty four hours of fighting between the Confederated Earth Forces and the Invy.

Interlude

CEF HQ, Raven Rock

"This is all we have?" barked Bob Dalpe at the junior enlisted who brought him a small cup of coffee.

"I'm sorry, Sir, but this is the very last of the frozen stuff. Our last shipment from the silverbacks in Jamaica, well your staff used that up last week." The girl was young, one of those recruited from the ruins, and didn't understand coffee.

"Leave her alone, General," laughed Colonel Jameson, the Air Wing CO. "She's scared out of her wits working around you as it is."

"How the hell am I supposed to fight a war without any coffee?" he barked back.

"We aren't fighting, they are," motioned the former fighter pilot, a vague hand wave indicating, 'out there'.

Dalpe snorted, sipped some of the horrible coffee, and dismissed the enlisted woman. Together with his command staff, they watched the clock countdown to H Hour, the seconds seeming to drag. When it finally clicked over to 12:00 Zulu time, 06:00 on the East Coast, Dalpe let out a breath that he didn't know he had been holding. Eleven years of hiding, nine years of occupation, it all came down to this moment, though elements of the CEF had been moving for hours already, planes and missiles launched minutes ago.

He crossed himself, made a silent prayer for victory, and got to work.

Chapter 47

Warrens' consciousness had expanded when he was jacked in, and he touched every sensor, every quantum entanglement, and every communications node left to the CEF forces. Far fewer than when they had fought their original battle, with only one ship to command. Still, he felt magnified, almost godlike as he thought of his plan.

"Hubris, General, is what got us to the place we are," said a voice, bringing him back down to semblance of reality.

"Thank you, Lex," he answered, "we won't make that mistake this time." In return he felt the artificial intelligence that lived in the half wrecked fleet carrier *U.S.S. Lexington* smile.

He wondered what it had been like for her, drifting for eleven years in space, slowly working to repair her own damage after being abandoned by her human crew. Though the avatar of the AI, and much of her personality, had been modeled after her captain, Kira Arkady, Lady Lex was also the ship, and her damage was her own pain.

"I wish we had Hal with us," he unconsciously uttered. The other surviving AI, who had lived in the Command and Control nodes of the CEF, had disappeared five minutes ago, locked in combat with the Invy AI that ran their networks. They would see him again soon, or never.

"General, my sensors have detected that the two Invy cruisers at Titan have ignited their engines, and are accelerating at twenty gravities towards Earth intercept, separated from each other by only two kilometers. It is a standard tactic we saw in the battle, to confuse sensors."

"Twenty G? They aren't going to be able to keep that up for long, it will kill the crew," he answered.

"Probably for at least an hour, then they will drop back to a more reasonable acceleration. Even so, they will have considerable speed and a quick intercept."

"And their Lunar Base?" asked Warren.

Lex waited a moment before responding, *"I will not know their reaction for several minutes. CEF radio intercept at Raven Rock indicates increased traffic. Wait ..."* and her voice cut off.

After a minute, she came back online. *"Ansible from Cascades Base indicates Station Two has been attacked by our Pacific based submarines. They are giving the go order for ground units."*

A cold sweat broke out on Warren. It was up to him now; if they failed to stop the incoming cruisers, then they were done. They had orbital bombardment systems, just as the stations did, and no matter what victories the CEF scored on the ground, space was what ultimately mattered.

"OK, here we go, Lex," he said. "We're going to go for an up the skirt shot on their engines at their flip with your rail gun. Do you think you can do it? Their fusion drives will be blinding them to your position, but we have a very small angle." His intent was to hit them just as they turned over to place their drives in front, allowing for deceleration and arrival at Earth orbit.

"It depends on their speed at that point. In effect, the combined velocity will be close to a fraction of C, and from my study of their shielding, the window will be approximately fifteen meters wide."

Holy crap. They were going to try to hit two passing targets, at an angle to the *Lexington's* position, moving at unknown speed approaching a fraction of the speed of light, with a rail gun that might or might not work.

"Easier than bulls eying womp rats back home on Tattoine," he said, and was surprised when the AI laughed.

"May the Force be with you, General," she said in her rough voice.

"And with you! Because we're going to need it. Let's assume we get one, but not the other. Options?"

"We close with and defeat the enemy."

Well, there's always that, he thought. "I'm going to assume we miss both, thought we still try for it. Here's what I want you to do. Do you know of Odysseus?"

"General, I am an AI. I had the entirety of the internet to learn from. Though I still do not understand your species fascination with viewing sexual reproduction."

"I'm surprised you still think we're worth saving," he answered. "OK, so we're going to pull a Trojan Horse, sort of, or more like a sucker punch. I want those fighters you have in your bay lit up, and they're going to go for the wormhole. Threaten that, and they're going to shit themselves; it's their communication with the rest of the Invy Empire."

"But what is the Trojan horse part?" the AI asked.

"That other fighter, the one trailing you. That's going to be sitting waiting for them along their intercept course for the wormhole. We're going to detonate it just as they go past, and THEN hit them with your railgun. But you will have to carefully maneuver to get yourself in position, or, go balls to the wall with acceleration to catch up to them. The two fighters will destroy the wormhole junction with their nukes. If we don't cut that off, we're going to have another Invy fleet on us, and none of this will matter."

"The mathematics will necessitate me cutting myself off from you while I compute. I will have a solution in approximately twenty five hours, once I know their speed and vector."

"Lex, Kira trusted you, and I trust you. I will wait."

She nodded, and her avatar, looking so much like his lost love, her captain, smiled, and then blinked out. David Warren was left to sit in his command chair, to wait out the first day of the war, unable, and unwilling to influence the events that he had set into motion.

While he waited, he thought about the Invy, trying to figure them out. There were three races that he knew of, and probably more that he didn't. In his mind, courtesy of the implant, he held terabytes of data, all the information the CEF had on them. Each called themselves by their own name in their language, but he knew them by their human nicknames. Dragons, the leadership, six limbed and reptilian. They ruled an interstellar empire of eleven enslaved worlds, using wormhole technology to move their ships. Wolverines, their uplifted infantry, wolf-like creatures who were tough and vicious, yet honorable in their own way. Last, the mysterious Octos, looking for all the world like an Earth octopus on land, managing the Invy tech.

The question he couldn't get out of his head was, one that had bothered him for all of his long exile, was simply, "Why?" None of it made any sense. Sure, the Invy had somewhat superior technology, but only about a century ahead of earth. The odds of two species being that close to each other, only light years away, was astronomical. Even more, the Dragons' rule was apparently feudally based, hardly something that catered to innovation and technological development. Their fleet went from world to world, hammering them into submission, and then moved on, as far as CEF Intelligence could tell. Individual aliens came to carve out domains, and establish cities in the tropics. That was pretty much all they knew about their culture.

Another thing that puzzled him was the charade they played, trying to brainwash humans into believing they were there to "rescue" Earth from environmental degradation. In reality, it was slavery marked by stagnation and slaughter. He had access to the interrogation reports from the CEF xenobiologist, Doctor Morano, from the one Dragon they had ever been able to take alive. Inwardly he cursed at her; she had killed it to do an autopsy. Warren would have loved to have his own interrogation session with the creature, but maybe after today they would have more opportunity.

None of it made any sense, but he still passed the time waiting trying to puzzle it out. Like soldiers throughout the ages, he had plenty of time to sit and think before the action started.

Part II

"…when the band begins to play."
Outside Loch Brea Invy Spaceport, Scotland.

Chapter 48

"For it's Tommy this, an' Tommy that, an 'Chuck him out, the brute!' But it's 'Saviour of 'is country' when the guns begin to shoot!" muttered Private Thomas Atkins as he looked through his rifle scope. He wasn't watching any of the enemy; instead he was gauging wind speed and direction between himself and the sensor pod mounted on a tower high above the base. In his hands he held a .50 caliber rifle with high explosive rounds.

"That's why your mother named you Tommy, son. So you can die for your King and Country!" said Sergeant Vlonski as he lay next to him. The polish immigrant still spoke with a heavy accent, but was as laconic as his native English counterparts.

"I bloody hope not, but if I do, the girls in Inverness will burn down the Invy town all on their own," he replied with a grin.

Private Fiona McClellan watched the rear approach. Like them, she was under an IR blanket, heat being converted into electricity and discharging slowly into the ground via a lead to a stake. She looked again at her watch; H-Hour minus one. In less than a minute, Atkins would put several rounds into the sensor pod. If the Russian submarines had done their job, the orbital approaching the U.K. would be blinded, giving them a half hour or more window to attack; destroying the sensor would blind the base defenses.

McClellan thought again about how she had wound up here, sweating her ass off in the cool October sun, machine gun in her hands. She had been finishing college, almost ready to become an accountant, when the Invy came, and now she was the mother of one child, with her husband in the actual assault force. Never would have met him if the Invy hadn't come, she mused. Probably never going to see him again if this doesn't work, either.

Atkins was a perpetual complainer, but knew his job well. Though he'd never actually fired on the Invy before, his team regularly hunted the bandits who preyed on small homesteads, in the social anarchy that was once the United Kingdom. Twenty now, he'd known nothing but the occupation, but still resented the life that had been denied him, one that he could barely remember.

"Where the hell is Thog?" the sniper asked Vlonski. The NCO shrugged; the uplifted ape did what he wanted to do, and more often than not, it was something useful. Instead he thought about how he himself had wound up there, stranger in a strange land. He had had no communication with his homeland in more than ten years, and didn't know if his wife and children were still alive. What had been a month-long job working on the London docks had turned into eleven years of fighting and killing, and soon, he promised himself, it would be all over.

"Do you see anything?" he asked Atkins. The younger man had shifted his scope to follow the path of the scout team that was positioning to seize the assault shuttle.

The sniper waited a moment before answering, "I THINK I saw a bit of movement by the port perimeter fence, but I can't be sure. Between those bloody chameleon suits and their skill, I doubt I'd catch anything that might give me a shot. And they're under the blackout cone of the sensor pod tower."

For all his bravery, Vlonski knew that what the scouts were doing took a kind of courage that he didn't have. Each member of the infiltration team was former Special Air Service, Royal Marine Commando, or Special Boat Service. Even more, the two pilots that accompanied them, well, they must have had a serious set of brass balls. To steal an aircraft they had only flown in simulators, with alien controls, fly it nap of the earth, probably under fire, pick up an assault team, and hurtle themselves into space! And yet the CEF commanders and soldiers around him acted as if it were just, as the Americans used to say on TV, a walk in the park.

He looked again at his watch.

H-0:00

Chapter 49

"And Fire, Fire, Fire!" muttered Sergeant Vlonski. Atkins breathed out, and gently squeezed the Barret's trigger. The big rifle rocked back on his shoulder, and he grunted with the effort to keep it on target. He was tempted to fire another round, but the impact of the bullet, two seconds after he pulled the trigger, shattered the sensor ball. Immediately sirens started to sound on the base, and he moved to his alternate firing position, this one pointed down into the base. It was time to go Dragon hunting.

"Twelve hundred yards, HQ building, exiting doorway," called the Sergeant, wide angle spotter scope glued to his eye. Atkins shifted to the right, and caught sight of the gold armor as the Invy used all six legs to run for the airfield. The ruling Invy resembled nothing so much as an upright Komodo Dragon, but were highly intelligent and more vicious. He led the target by almost twenty feet, then thirty; the bastards were fast. BOOM! and the rifle kicked again, jumping off the sandbags. It hammered into the creature and sent it spinning across the runway.

"Eight hundred yards, pilot ready room, side doors," and again the rifle boomed, once, twice, three times.

"TIME TO GO, LADS!' called Private McClellan, her voice pitched high with excitement and adrenaline. The bases' automated counter sniper sensor would be coming back online, degraded without the sensor mount, but still accurate enough. Their next alternate site was a hundred meters to the left, and they hustled behind the ridge line to make it there. Every second spent outside a firing spot was more time for the Invy to get their shite together. They had just turned around a corner of the trail when their old site melted under concerted plasma cannon fire, the explosion lighting up the afternoon sky, and the shock wave making them stumble as they ran.

"Bloody Main Force buggers better start their damned attack!" grunted Atkins as he snaked his way forward, careful not to hit the scope of the rifle on anything. At this range, even the slightest jarring would throw his shot off by feet instead of inches.

"Ours is not to…" started Vlonski, with a grin, his Polish accent thick with excitement.

"Oh shut yer bloody pie hole, you foreign bastard," said Atkins, placing his cheek to the stock. The sergeant put the spotter scope to his eye, and started to scan for targets. Below them the base looked like an anthill that had been kicked open.

"Take out that mortar, thirteen hundred yards, left of the HQ." Three Wolverines were just visible inside the sandbagged emplacement, moving the heavy mortar around in a circle, angling it towards the south. From that direction they all could hear the gunfire erupting as the Main Force battalion assaulted the base. He lined the scope up on the top of the mortar tube, checked the wind, and fired. This time, he waited for the scope to settle again and checked the results, which were only a huge cloud of dust as the heavy round hit a sandbag. On target, but slightly low. The Wolverines had immediately ducked behind the wall, and his next shot shattered the mortar and sent the tube spinning up in the air. Atkins would have liked to put a few rounds in the short, upright, nasty wolf like creatures, the Uplifted the Dragons used as their infantry, but that wasn't his mission today.

He jumped when gunfire, a long burst from McClellan's' SAW, erupted behind him. Plasma bolts cracked in return, and the shots stopped, replaced with her screaming as if her soul was on fire, mixed with excited barks of Invy troops tearing into her flesh. Vlonski grabbed the sniper and bodily threw him forward, down the slope. Atkins wrapped himself around the rifle as he fell, finally slamming into a tree. He started to get back up, dropping the big gun and clawing at his pistol, even as the Pole slid down next to him, followed by several shots from plasma rifles. As his Sergeant half ran, half slid past, Atkins fired back up the hill, then turned and ran after him, grabbing the rifle, towards the gully below.

They ducked down behind the first rock outcropping that showed, and paused to catch their breath. Vlonski's blonde hair was matted to his head, and he groaned softly, holding his leg. Through his jeans showed an ugly burn where a bolt had scored the muscle.

"Fiona?" asked Atkins.

Vlonski shook his head, gritted his teeth, and said, "Random Wolverine patrol, bad luck for us, worse luck for her."

An Invy shuttle rocketed overhead, just barely clearing the trees, headed west. Both flinched, not knowing if it was the one supposed to be stolen. It didn't matter, though, because they had more pressing things to worry about. From uphill came the excited yips and barks of the patrol, searching for them.

"We gotta move, mate, can you walk? If the Main Force can take the base, we can get these bloody dogs off our backs and get you some help."

At that moment, their headsets crackled to life. *"All units, DUNKIRK DUNKIRK, DUNKIRK!"* and then fell silent. They both knew what that meant. The attack, never meant to be more than a diversion, was being called off.

"I knew that stupid thick headed Brigadier didn't have the balls to carry it off," said the Sergeant. "If it were a Polish general in charge…"

"If it were a Pole, we'd be surrendering. Now we're up shit's creek, and this place is going to be swarming with Invy troops." He drew his pistol, and for a second, looked at Vlonski's wounded leg.

The NCO knew what the sniper was thinking. "You don't have to shoot me. I'll stay and hold them off. Go and get yourself out of here, and kill some more of the bastards."

Instead, Atkins grabbed him, slung the bigger mans' arm over his shoulder, and started to jog at an angle, trying to keep the rock outcropping between them and the searching patrol. He knew they didn't have a chance in hell; the doggies were out for blood, probably with their noses pressed to the ground, tracking them. Grunting with the effort, he took a second to holster the pistol and reach into his pocket. Tearing at the packet with his teeth, Atkins dumped a whole cup of cayenne pepper on the ground.

"Sniff that trail, you cunts," he said, and they tried to pick up the pace. Vlonski was becoming more a dead weight as the pain hobbled him, blood seeping from his leg muscles and nicked artery.

Chapter 50

They could hear the barks behind them, and Atkins had a pretty good feeling they were done for. Vlonski was trying to help himself along, but he was going into shock from his wound.

"You know," said the sniper, "I don't really like you, you stupid Pollack. You're too much of a hard ass, mate."

"Then put me down, shit for brains, and get yourself away," he answered, trying to shrug off the younger man's grip. Their situation was made moot, however, as the Wolverines sighted them, started barking furiously, and laid down a barrage of plasma fire. Atkins knew that several would be maneuvering through the brush to get into hand to hand range, and frigging eat them alive.

"Not bloody likely!" he muttered, rolled over, and lining the scope of the big gun up through the brush, fired. The round plowed into the dirt at the feet of the furthest Invy, and Atkins cursed. The sight had been knocked out of alignment by the fall; he corrected and fired again, even as the plasma crept closer and closer. One of the creatures seemed to disappear in an explosion of blood and gore, and the others went to cover.

From the side, Vlonski emptied his pistol at four of the enemy who had appeared out of the tree line, twenty meters away, and running all out. He hit one, the small bullet scoring the creature's flank, and then the slide locked back. Atkins turned to fire, rolling on his back and looking down the barrel, and the Barrett barked once, then was torn from his hands as a grey furred Invy howled and jumped on him, driving its ripping claw down deep into his shoulder.

The soldier screamed with pain and rage, and was answered by a deep grunting sound, as a huge silver and black creature charged past him, massive hand swatting the Wolverine off. The uplifted gorilla hammered into the patrol, scattering their much smaller bodies, killing two with the double bladed axe he carried in one massive fist The third he ripped apart with his bare hands, and then the silverback turned to the last one. No coward, the Wolverine charged, and they came together in a clash of jaws and fangs, but the massive bulk of the human's ally easily hammered the Invy into the ground. He jumped up and down on it several times, flattening the corpse, then howled and beat his chest, yelling out a challenge to the remaining Invy, a hundred meters away. There was no answer; the ones firing the plasma had run at the sight of the bull ape.

"Mother Mary of God, am I happy to see you, Corporal Thog!" said Atkins, over the pain of his wound.

The ape grunted, muttered "COME!" and made the signs for them to follow. Then he said, "Where Fi?"

"She bought it, mate. Saved our lives though; crap this hurts."

The ape was silent for a moment, then grunted "Heal," and dragged out a medical kit from the harness he wore. Vlonski grabbed at it, pulled out a bandage and pressed it to Atkins' shoulder. The embedded nanos started clotting right way, and Atkins felt instantly better. In return, he did the same for the Pole's leg. Not waiting for them, Thog gathered up each under a great hairy arm, and started off on a loping run through the forest.

They caught up with the retreating main body in an hour, though they didn't rejoin them. As they crested a hill, Invy attack aircraft screamed overhead, and delivered a flurry of plasma shots at the column of bedraggled troops. Return fire downed one of the craft, but the others pounced on the antiaircraft position, hammering it and drawing secondary explosions. They could hear the screams of wounded echoing through the valley, faint between gunfire and explosions.

"Holy shite!" said Atkins, and Vlonski grunted in agreement. Even as they watched, the troops below them broke and ran. At the head of the valley, blocking their line of retreat, five Invy transports grounded, ramps thundered down, and Wolverines spilled out of them.

The Invy started hunting individuals, and the best troops of the CEF in Europe were slaughtered, or chased off. "Time to bug out, Thog. Go back to your people, this is not your fight," said Vlonski.

"Thog stay, hunt Invy," grunted the ape, and he picked them up again, moving swiftly and silently away from the scene of the battle. Neither man understood why the Uplifted of Earth helped the CEF, though Thog had tried to explain once in his abbreviated, limited way.

"Ape equal man now. Invy no make free, make Thog's people slaves," the silverback had grunted, and then said no more on the matter.

Their trip back to the base took almost the entire day, resting briefly, avoiding Invy air patrols, and it was full dark when they finally got in sight of the HQ, hidden no longer. It still held out, but not for long; Invy armor was hammering the entrance to the cave complex. Even as they watched, a heavy plasma cannon was fired at the main doors, bursting them open, and hundreds of Wolverines surged in through the entrance.

"Well, now what?" asked Atkins. Vlonski was his Sergeant, but did that even matter now?

Thog grunted, and pointed up. "No moving stars falling," he signed. Though the uplifted had augmented intelligence, it was often difficult to form human speech, and the apes signed as much as spoke.

"You are right, my friend," said the Pole and he started to laugh. The ape grunted in amusement with him.

"What the bloody hell are you laughing at?" asked Atkins, thoroughly confused.

Vlonski said, "No orbital strikes! We hurt them, hurt them bad." The sky was cloudy, so they couldn't see anything above, tell how many orbitals were left, but the ape was right.

"So now what?" asked the sniper.

"Now, we are going to make their lives hell. Don't you Scots have a history of being a pain in the ass to occupiers?"

"I'm not a damn Scot, and you know that, but yes, they are a bloody pain in the ass," said the man from Liverpool.

Their conversation was interrupted by a group of people coming down the road, slowly, silently. They were civilians, refugees from one of the towns. A man, a woman, and child, shuffling slowly through the night.

"Hey!" said Atkins. "Where are you lot going? There's fighting up ahead!"

The man looked at him, stared at his CEF uniform, and swung his fist at the sniper, catching the surprised soldier in the face. Vlonski waved Thog off and grabbed the man in a bear hug, ignoring his own wounds, even as the woman stood dully by and said nothing.

With a curse, the civilian shook Vlonski off, and said harshly, "We nae asked for this, soldier boy, and now look what yea done! My baby is dead, and our home gone."

"Blame it on the Invy, you bastard," said Atkins, spitting put blood.

"No," answered the woman, scorn in her voice. "If ye'ad won, that would be one thing, but yea lost, ya stupid soldiers. Look at ya, in your fancy uniforms. Yea can go to hell." Then she spit on him, and the family turned and walked into the darkness.

"Never changes," said Private Tommy Atkins, in a bitter voice.

Chapter 51

They made it to a backup rally point outside the Invy town of Inverness before dawn, giving sign and countersign at the entrance to the old castle. What reassured the nervous sentry, more than their answers, was the hulking bulk of Thog.

"Right," said the ranking officer there, Captain MacIvers, staring at a map. "You two make eleven, and yon beastie will be a huge help. Have you got any weapons?"

"My Barrett, but I only have three rounds left, and my sight is off. What the hell happened, Sir?"

The Scot scowled, and cursed a blue streak. "What happened, is that stupid Sassenach General Walters lost his nerve, and ordered a pullback just as we became decisively engaged. We HAD them, and the stupid git got a lot of good men slaughtered."

"So what do we do now?" asked Vlonski.

"Sergeant, we are going to make ourselves a huge pain in the Invy's ass. We have no communications with any higher headquarters, but we have to assume that, with the lack of orbital strikes, things are moving forward."

"Until what? The Americans show up here with a huge bloody fleet and save our asses?" asked Atkins.

"Private," said MacIvers, "we fight until they do, or until we're all dead. Do you understand what they're doing in the Invy towns right now?" Neither man had any idea, and said so.

"They're shooting one in ten right now as punishment, and killing everyone in the villages close to the base," said the Captain. "So we are going to kill as many Invy as we can, as fast as we can. Now, go rest up, I've got work to do and you're both wounded. Sergeant Vlonski, until someone else shows up with more experience, you are the acting platoon sergeant. I expect others will return in the night. Dismissed."

Atkins grumbled as they found a room and sat to eat some food. Thog was not in evidence; the ape didn't care much for human company if he could avoid it.

"Bloody uptight wanker, that Captain," said Atkins as he chewed a cold sausage. "Makes my sainted dead bitchy mum look like a breath of bloody fresh air."

Vlonski nodded, and said, "I would not want his job; he needs to motivate everyone to keep fighting."

"Well, it's not like we have any choice," said Atkins. At that moment, they were interrupted by a man who barged in through the blanket over the door.

"Tommy!" barked the wild eyed soldier at Atkins, "Where the hell is Fiona!" He was burly, dark haired, and wore a tattered camouflaged kilt. His face was burned and dirty, and scorch marks extended across his armor and under a bloody bandage.

Despite his own wound, Vlonski stood up and grabbed David McClellan in a bear hug as the man looked about wildly. "Go home, Davey. Go home to your kid," he said calmly. The man's face tightened, and he closed his eyes in a grimace of grief.

"She's dead, isn't she?" said the man, over sobs.

"Aye, mate, saved our lives. Do like Ski said, go home to your kid," said Atkins.

"I've got no home anymore," was the wretched answer. "They killed everyone in the village."

None of the three men said anything more, Vlonski just held onto the Scot as he slowly crumpled. After a time, McClellan looked up and said dully, "I'm going to kill them all."

"Yes," said the Pole, who didn't even know if his family was alive. "We're going to."

The watch on Sergeant Vlonski's wrist flipped over to zero hundred hours; a new day had begun.

Part III
"Death is light as a feather"
CEF HQ, Japan

The soldier and sailor should consider loyalty their essential duty. Who that is born in this land can be wanting in the spirit of grateful service to it? No soldier or sailor, especially, can be considered efficient unless this spirit be strong within him. A soldier or a sailor in whom this spirit is not strong, however skilled in art or proficient in science, is a mere puppet; and a body of soldiers or sailors wanting in loyalty, however well-ordered and disciplined it may be, is in an emergency no better than a rabble. Remember that, as the protection of the state and the maintenance of its power depend upon the strength of its arms, the growth or decline of this strength must affect the nation's destiny for good or for evil; therefore neither be led astray by current opinions nor meddle in politics, but with single heart fulfill your essential duty of loyalty, and bear in mind that duty is weightier than a mountain, while death is lighter than a feather. Never, by failing in moral principle, fall into disgrace and bring dishonor upon your name.

~Gunjin Chokuyu, 1892 (Imperial Rescript to Soldiers and Sailors)

Chapter 52

Before the Invasion, she had been a fighter pilot, flying for the Japanese Defense Forces, becoming their first "Ace" in almost a hundred years over the South China Sea. Then, soon afterwards, due to her very distant connection to the Imperial Throne, and the death of the entire royal family, Captain Kiyomi Ichijou had become Empress Kiyomi. Through nine long years of occupation, she had shepherded her people, keeping the peace with the Invy while fostering the strength of the hidden Confederated Earth Forces units on her islands. Now, though, now she wanted to become unbound from the earth, to climb skyward and bring death to the enemies of her people, and of all mankind.

"Colonel, we need those planes up ASAP!" said the Raptor pilot.

"Am I talking to Captain Ichijou, or the Empress?"

"Both!" she answered, "And it is MY ass, and my pilots, and my subjects, that are depending on you, my Chief of Maintenance. Now I need ten planes, fully armed and fueled in ten minutes!"

The man went away grumbling, and she smiled. Ten was far too many, considering the lack of spare parts and the age of the planes, some almost fifty years old. Six would be enough, based on the scouts' report of Cam Ranh Bay's airfield. She expected four Invy fighters; more could come, but their mission would be over by then. Still, she had to push him.

She climbed up the ladder to her plane, and ran her hand over the five Chinese and two Russian flags painted under her name. The Spratly War had been fought even after the Invy Scout had crashed and the push had been on to form the CEF. She had been just twenty-three, fresh out of the academy, and Japan's hero, if only for a moment.

As she lowered the canopy and started the engines, her crew chief gave her a thumbs up; Captain Ichijou returned it. Then he bowed, and fled down the ladder, even as others pulled it away from the rumbling F-22. She looked over and saw the maintenance officer, who held up seven fingers. That would have to do.

The next step on her checklist gave her pause. In place of the 20mm rotary cannon, an Invy anti-tank caliber plasma gun had been retrofitted into her weapons suite. Of course they had never been able to test it on a moving, flying aircraft, but she would have to remember that the muzzle velocity on the weapons rendered the leading of the target negligible.

Ahead, the massive doors concealed in the side of the mountain slowly slid open, revealing the last rays of sunset. She would have preferred the sight of a rising sun, but this would have to do. The pilot slowly increased her thrust, rolling the plane forward, gently working the rudder pedals and brakes to line up with the now wide-open doorway.

When the fighter plane cleared the entrance, she pushed the throttles forward while standing on the brakes. As much as the fighter pilot in her wanted to hit afterburners and rocket down the highway, Kiyomi Ichijou knew that it would be a waste of precious fuel. Instead, once all seven planes of her flight, two F-22s and five of the Japanese version of the venerable F-16, called that they were clear of the doors, she let the brakes go and increased thrust.

The vibration of the engines coursed through her body, and acceleration pushed her back in her seat. She yelled with joy as the front wheels left the ground, and that blissful feeling of being airborne again enveloped her, back in her true element.

Behind her, one of the F-16s suddenly dropped out of the air, several hundred feet off the ground and at several hundred miles per hour. It crashed in a fireball of burning jet fuel, and no chute appeared. Her joy was tempered by their first casualty as she watched it in her rear facing camera, and she said a silent prayer for the man, another good friend.

They flew low over the ocean, at an easy six hundred knots, towards what had been dubbed "Yankee Station", the place where the submarines were to launch. She wished desperately for an AWACS radar plane to vector them in. Even as they approached, she saw the first series of contrails leaping from the ocean as the missiles reached up for the Invy orbital.

Her call was the first radio traffic to have been heard on Earth in more than a decade. *"For your Empress, for our ancestors, and for us all, let's do this! Sixteen element, stay and cover the submarines. Remember, their interceptors are not really designed for atmosphere. We can out maneuver them. KEEP THEM OFF THE SUBS! Meinu,"* she called to her wingman, *"follow me on high altitude intercept."*

The Raptor leapt upwards, finally set free, almost wingtip to wingtip with her partner. Climbing higher and higher, the sky started to darken before they tipped over and leveled out. She activated the AN/APG-77 radar, giving up the F-22's stealth advantage out of necessity, and immediately got a return, 327 km out, approaching at a closing speed of almost three thousand kph.

"TALLYHO! Six, no, eight Invy approaching at angels 30! Vector 195 degrees, engaging!" The call was for the benefit of the older F-16s, which didn't have the data link the F-22s shared.

Captain Kiyomi Ichijou, set free from the burden of being Empress, dove at the enemy of her world with a fierce, exultant joy in her heart. Even as she did, far to the southwest, another sun blazed forth, and she screamed "BANZAI!!!!" into the radio, and loosed a pair of AMRAAM missiles, the first shots of taking back Earth, or dying out as a race.

Never mind that it was a nuclear weapon; she had her Rising Sun.

Chapter 53

When you pull a high G turn, things happen to your body. Depending on which way you're turning, blood is forced to your head, or down to your feet. Either way, you can black out, from too much blood, or not enough. G suits help, squeezing the blood back up to your body, to your heart. So does clamping down on your muscles, grunting with effort as you try to wrestle with the controls of your plane. Fighting the stick, while trying to keep situational awareness, watching your radar for the enemy. Scanning X, Y, Z axis and time, calculating fuel, listening to your computer scream warnings in your ear about the damage your plane has suffered.

"Jiko, he's on my ass and my ailerons are damaged!" called her wingman.

"Hold tight, Meinu, I'm on my way. Give me a scissor left to drag him into my sights!"

Captain Kiyomi Ichijou slammed her F-22 hard right, gaining speed as she tilted downward, lining up for the shot as blue plasma bolts zipped past her canopy. Her wingman rolled desperately, trying to lead the Invy fighter into Ichijou's sights. She held it a bit too long, and the plane disappeared in a fire ball, just as her commander blew the tail off the Invy fighter.

The Empress cursed, rolling hard and hitting afterburners, diving towards the sea as more plasma bolts ripped by her. At the bottom of her dive, she leveled out barely ten feet above the waves, then cursed at herself. The Invy fighter worked on antigravity, and had no intakes to ingest spray and flame out. On the other hand, they weren't as maneuverable as the fifth generation fighter plane, and she screamed again with joy as the alien ship failed to level out and plowed into the sea.

Hauling back on the stick, she searched the skies and her display at the same time. In the distance, a hundred kilometers away, radar showed multiple tracks as her F-16's tried to keep the remaining Invy off the submarines. Watching her fuel gauge, she made up her mind. Her plane was worth far less than one of the few precious subs, still firing their payload of surface to space nukes at the orbital stations. She pushed the throttle down, dumping fuel into the engines, and rocketed forward, already far past the speed of sound.

The radio crackled into life as she launched her last AMRAAM from fifty klicks out. It leapt away from her plane and tracked unerringly into the second to last Invy, leaving just one alien ship in the sky, and one Japanese fighter. The area was covered in smoke from the surface to space missiles fired by the American submarines, and she lined up to take the shot as it disappeared in to the clouds. Her HUD display showed the infrared signature of the ship, not as hot as a jet, but bleeding red from the air friction on the edges of its wings. Behind it and above was the white hot flare of a CEF fighter.

"Jiko, I'm out of missiles, and Winchester on guns," called the F-16 pilot.

The F-22 started to vibrate, almost imperceptibly at first, then growing noticeably. The first Invy interceptor she had tagged had scored a plasma bolt in the head on pass, and bits of her plane's skin had been shedding throughout the fight. Now, at supercruise, more than a thousand miles per hour, structural members were being exposed, and her airstream was being disturbed, creating a vicious loop that tore away more of her fuselage.

Closer. Closer. Closer. She didn't know the range of the plasma cannon they had jury rigged in the nose of her fighter, but she assumed it was line of sight. Her first rounds tracked towards the ship as it headed towards the center of the ring of subs, and she grinned slightly, the exaltation of the kill and victory coursing through her veins.

With the third shot, the cannon stopped firing, and the emergency overheat lights flashed on her HUD, along with the other warnings. The plane was vibrating like crazy, and she dropped her speed below the sound barrier as the shaking got worse. Even as she broke through the clouds of smoke, she saw the Invy ship in front of her.

"Empress," called the F-16 pilot as his plane arched over in a dive that far exceeded the max speed of the fifty year old fighter, *"I go to glory! Remember me!"*

"I shall, Hayoto, I shall," she whispered into the radio.

A glowing light dropped from the Invy interceptor and fell in an arc towards the ocean, even as the last F-16 plowed into it, and both exploded in a flash of antimatter. The light hit the water, sank for a few seconds, and then the surface of the sea leapt upwards, a huge circle a kilometer across rose up for her plane.

Ichijou broke left, for Japan and home, dumping fuel into her afterburners and clawing for altitude. There was a loud BANG! from behind her, and alarms started to scream. Glancing at the rear view plasma screen, through the flickering image she saw that she had left the circle of disturbed water behind. Ichijou leveled the plane out as the vibration turned into a violent shaking.

Hitting full flaps to bleed off speed, the veteran pilot waited until the air speed indicator read only three hundred knots, despite the violent shaking, despite the desperate desire to punch out as fast as possible. Reaching one hand down between her legs and tucking the other in tight, she felt around for the ejection handle, gripped it, and pulled. The canopy bolts blew and the airstream hammered into her, even as the rocket under the seat ignited. She grunted as the seat was blasted upward, arched, and then she fell outward and away, the drogue chute pulling the main out.

As the Empress drifted downward, she looked toward the sky, and thanked the gods that her helmet visor was down. In the blueness flashed a light bright enough to compete with the sun overhead. It was followed by an even bigger explosion, as the main antimatter reactor on the Invy orbital went critical and detonated.

Time. They had given the ground forces time.

Chapter 54

Being Empress of Japan doesn't really do squat for you when you're floating in a life raft, hundreds of miles out to sea, thought Captain Ichijou. She laughed to herself, thinking of the airs she had sometimes put on when it had gone to her head.

The raft in question was floating in a sea of dead and stunned fish, for which she was grateful. A phobia of sharks had followed her since watching "Jaws" as a child, and she had scrambled up into the raft almost before her flight suit had soaked through. To her sorrow, she also saw many dead dolphins, and in the distance, the bodies of several whales bobbed to the surface. The concussive effect of the anti-matter depth charge must have been enormous, and she wondered about the submarines.

In the sky overhead, the afterglow of the station detonating had vanished, but she still had to worry about sunburn when the sun rose. Next step was inventory of what she had in order to survive. Water, of course. She had about a gallon of it tucked in various pockets, and there was a distiller in the survival kit. Food wouldn't be a problem for a while with all the dead fish.

She pulled out the clicker, a metal object about the length of her middle finger that, when twisted, would make a CLICK that would be audible for miles underwater, calling any dolphins nearby. Called a "Burrill", it had been named after its inventor, a US Navy C-130 crewman who had transitioned to working with the Cetaceans. She had never had to use it before, although some of the Scout teams did to call them in to the shore. In addition there was a battery powered sonar pinger to guide any subs to her position. For some reason the dolphins always ignored them, like they did many electrical powered devices.

Looking around at all the dead mammals, she zipped the Burrill back in her pocket, deployed the sonar beacon, and sat trying to figure out how far from the epicenter she had travelled before bailing out. More than fifty kilometers, more or less, at the speed she had been going. Hopefully some of the submarines had made it out OK; there was still a war to be fought.

Overhead, she watched as first one orbital crested the sky, and then disappeared. It was followed almost an hour later by another, so that meant there were two surviving. Who held them, she had no idea, but she thought she saw, before the second one disappeared over the eastern horizon, the telltale sparks of orbital strikes entering the atmosphere. When next they came around, there was nothing to see, just the lights moving through the sky.

Eventually, Ichijou found herself, well, bored. She floated on the gentle swells and a slight breeze pushed her eastward, away from the coast of Japan, hundreds of miles to the northwest. Every now and then the pilot placed the Burrill in the water and clicked it, but no response. She had come down from the adrenaline rush of air combat, and now, always the fighter pilot, grew restless, and actually concerned. If any kind of storm sprang up, the one man raft would be useless, and she would quickly drown. Ichijou would have given anything to know how the battle had gone, and was angry that she might die without knowing.

Suddenly, there was a bump on the bottom of the raft, and panic ran through her at the thought of a shark. The image of the little boy in Jaws flashed through her mind, getting swallowed whole on his raft by a giant Great White.

Instead, a grey, grinning head popped out of the sea, and started clicking and squealing furiously. Around the dolphins' body was a harness, with several odd bits of equipment strapped to it. She wondered if this was one of the US Navy's accompanying Cetaceans, and it was confirmed by a sleek tattoo on its skin, showing, of all things, Popeye the Sailor Man. In fact, the dolphin was covered in tattoos, now that she looked, some of them very crude. The mammal rolled over on (his?) side, displaying a box with a button, and the English language letters, "PUSH AND HOLD TO TALK."

She leaned over the raft, being careful not to slip out, and pushed. The dolphin burst out in an excited chatter, and the words sprang from a speaker. "HUMANS COME SKYBIRD FLY HUMANS COME DARWIN HEARS COME SOON MAKE READY!"

"Thank you, Darwin," she said, and clicks and squeals came back out of the box, but in her own voice. "Domo, Darwin. May you play forever in the seas!"

"KILL MANY MANY FAR SKY PEOPLES DARWIN FAMILY HELP ALL WHERE CAN!" came the reply, and her ally slipped beneath the waves.

Twenty minutes later, she heard it herself, the drone of airplane propellers, and her heart leapt inside her. The pilot took a pen flare from her harness, held it skyward, and fired it. The light arched up into the sky, and the pitch of the rotors changed. In a moment, a huge shape appeared in the darkness, a school bus sized fuselage slung between two enormous propellers.

The MV-22 Osprey slowed and rotated its wings to assume VTOL mode, and gently spun so that its rear facing ramp hovered over her. An orange clad para-rescue crewman swung down in a harness, to slowly settle into the water next to her.

"Are you injured?" he yelled over the rotor wash, and she shook her head no. He helped her put another harness under her shoulders, and the two were slowly winched upward and onto the ramp.

Another crewman helped her take the harness off, and there, standing on the deck, holding out a blanket, was Major Takara Ikeda. She let him wrap the blanket around her, and maybe leaned into him a little too hard, reveling in human contact. For a second, he dared to return the embrace, then seemed to awaken, hurriedly helping her strap in. As they climbed towards cruising speed, the Scout Team leader filled her in on the tactical and strategic situation.

As she changed out of her wet clothes, putting on a dry spare uniform, the Osprey thundered northward, forty year old airframe rattling like a garbage can being blown by a hurricane. Ichijou and Ikeda each plugged into the intercom, and Ikeda started talking.

"Two destroyed, one, well, disabled, one functional and in Invy control," he said, and watched for her reaction. She had none, just waited for him to continue.

"Station One you saw, I assume. Station Four blew to hell when the British tried to board it. Station Two is under control of the Americans, but the Invy scrambled the CPU, and locked it. So they can't operate any of the weapons systems. Their shuttle was holed, so they're stuck until one of two things happen."

"Go on," she said.

"Well, they have pilots, but no shuttles. We have two shuttles that we've captured, but…"

She finished for him, "No one qualified for Trans-atmospheric operations."

"Except yourself. Meanwhile, Station Four is still active. We either take our tech people to Station Two, or try to take Station Four."

At that, she looked directly at him. "Operation Dover?" she asked.

"The fake radio transmitters absorbed most of the missiles, but they also took out all the communications at the Cascades base, except the ansible. So they can't talk to the ground units in the Western US."

"I don't really care about that. The ground war in other parts of the world is not, right now, our problem. I am only concerned about Japan."

He said nothing, only looked away. "Tell me," she said, "Your Empress orders you."

Sighing, he answered, "Headquarters took over fifteen orbital strikes, heavies. It's gone. Maybe some of the lower levels, but the hangar is gone, and half the mountain collapsed inward."

Her people. Never mind the facility. Her people. "And now? What are they hitting now? The villages? How many have we taken?"

"Out of seventy eight Invy villages in Japan, eleven have reported secure. Fighting continues in thirty two, and we have no communication with seven. The remaining villages are in Invy hands."

"Civilian casualties?" Her people.

"Unknown at this time. Light, hopefully."

"Hope is not a plan, Takara, as the Americans say. Why no more orbital strikes?"

"We think they're out of weapons. The Americans have observed activity at Tyco crater, it's possible they are preparing to re-arm, probably within three hours."

"So we must stop them. And I am tired already." She leaned her head against the Major's shoulder, and in a moment, was fast asleep. He dared not move for the rest of the trip.

Chapter 55

They landed at a captured Invy space field, directly across from several Invy shuttles. Of the five originally there, two were smoking wrecks, one was missing, and two sat side by side. Around them lay bodies of Wolverines and Japanese CEF Main Force soldiers. With a jolt, the Osprey set down, and it woke up Ichijou. She sat up and looked wildly around before realizing where she was. Sheepishly, she wiped off some drool from her face, noticing that it had soaked into the Major's uniform.

"So, you see I am only human after all, Takara," she laughed.

He smiled, and said, "I never thought you were anything BUT human, Empress." He held her gaze, but flushed all the same. Her green eyes, so unusual for a pure Japanese, held him, and he felt himself grow hot.

"I forget myself, sometimes. Thank you," she said, and reached out to touch his face. Then it was her turn to grow flustered, and she turned and walked off down the ramp, hoping that he hadn't seen her own skin grow darker with a rush of blood. She felt like an idiot teenager.

"COLONEL!" she yelled at her logistics officer, who had come out to meet the VTOL. "I want both of those shuttles ready to go in half an hour. I don't care how you do it, but I want some kind of reflective or heat absorbing material on the bottom. YOU! Sergeant Major Shimata, GET OUR SOLDIERS BODIES OFF THIS GROUND!" The senior Noncom bowed low, and then started barking his own orders.

She was the Empress again, all humanity pushed aside as mission drove her forward. Turning back to Ikeda, she said, "Get a team together, rehearsal in fifteen minutes. Anyone who can fit in a suit."

He smiled, and bowed as low as the Sergeant Major had. She let a small grin slip, then turned away. The scout team commander already had his men ready to go; he had given orders as soon as the fighting here had stopped, telling his scouts to be prepped before he got back. They stood in the shade of the shuttle, some field stripping weapons and other sleeping, like soldiers from time immemorial.

Ikeda sat down and started working the knots out of his muscles. His second, Captain Bill Wallace, formerly of the Australian SAS, sat down next to him. Neither said anything for a minute, Wallace knowing that Ikeda would speak when necessary.

After the fight on the beach, the Japanese Scout Leader had put out a call for volunteers among the scout teams, and Wallace had shown up, along with three other Aussies and a New Zealander. All five had been caught in Japan, on an information exchange mission, when Southeast Asia command had gone silent from the 30 degree virus. They had been part of the infiltration of this base, losing several.

"Are the men ready?" asked Ikeda, eventually.

"Do dingos eat babies?" answered Wallace, with a straight face.

Ikeda grunted, and said, "That is not Australian, it is from an old American TV show. Seinfield."

"SeinFELD, mate."

It was a game the two played, trying to one up each other on American culture, and one Ikeda thoroughly enjoyed. "Whatever, dude," he answered, trying to unsettle the Aussie. Wallace just looked at him.

"So, are you prepared to die," said Ikeda, "in honorable service to your Empress?"

"Ain't my Empress! What I'm prepared to do, Major, is kick some Invy ass, and then take that shuttle and git back to Oz, you savvy? I'm not doing it for your future wife."

"My, my WHAT?" spluttered the Japanese, aghast.

Wallace laughed, "Well it's bloody obvious. The two of you dance round each other like a couple of dogs eyeing the same bone. Eventually one comes out on top, if you get my meaning."

The look Ikeda gave him made Wallace realize he had stepped over his bounds, but it was in his nature, once challenged, to push further. "We've got a bit of time before we lift, go tell her how you feel, mate. Last chance, maybe she'll bone you in the back of the shuttle."

"You disrespect me, and you disrespect my Empress," muttered the Major.

Wallace stood, and grinned. "Takara, you Japs are hell on wheels in a fight, but I have no idea how you ever get laid."

Ikeda looked over at where she was directing the installation of ablative covering over the bottom of the shuttle. Ichijou was tall for a Japanese woman; and her green eyes gave hint at some foreign ancestor long ago; her gaining the throne would have been impossible even twenty years ago. She was nothing like his dead wife, and the memory of her left him confused.

He got up and walked to a military storage container, calling for Sergeant Major Shimada. The NCO produced a key to match the one that Ikeda took from around his neck. Together, they opened the two locks, disarming the explosives inside. Shimada bowed, and walked away.

Ikeda took the long, canvas wrapped bundle from inside, and closed the lid again, automatically locking it. Then he walked over to Ichijou, and waited until she noticed him. When she did, he knelt on one knee. She was startled at his reaction, but her eyes opened even wider when she saw the wrapped object, and her breath hissed out from between her teeth.

"You may need this, Empress," he said, and handed it to her. She unwrapped it, and drew the sword from its sheath. For a moment, she said nothing. The sword was not in the traditional Katana style; it was older, and the blade looked almost like a short western broadsword. The bronze hilt was tarnished, but new leather bound the grip, and the steel shone in the sun.

"Kusanagi!" she whispered. Even she, the Empress of Japan, had never seen the blade that the Shinto priests guarded, only the wooden box it was kept in when she had been given her title.

"You may need it, and if we don't make it back, well, Japan will no longer be, well, Japan will no longer be. It is fitting."

He unbuckled his belt and give it to her, since she had none on her coverall, and the pilot slid it through the scabbard. Then he helped her buckle it around her hips, conscious of her waist in his hands, if even for a moment. Stepping back, the Major bowed low.

Around them, the flight crews and soldiers broke into a cheer, even the Australians joining in. It was, as the Americans say, hokey, but it felt right as she lifted the blade in the air, the rising sun catching the ancient steel of the sword of the Divine Rulers of Japan.

Chapter 56

From the cockpit, Captain Ichijou called back into the troop compartment. "Station coming over the horizon, and we're going to be exceeding the inertial compensator as I maneuver. Strap in."

"Uh, what?" said one of the Aussies, looking at the seats designed for the smaller Wolverines.

Wallace grinned at him, lay flat on the floor, and wrapped a strap around his arm, first securing his weapons. "Just hang on tight, Johnnie!"

As he said it, the pilot shouted, "MISSILES INCOMING!' and the craft pitched violently over to one side in a ten gravity turn, damped down to a punishing five, and the soldiers were thrown about, hanging on for dear life. Then they were weightless, then tossed towards the rear of the craft. Only the superb training and shape they were in allowed them to withstand the violent maneuvering. A pallet of gear broke loose and crashed into one of the Japanese soldiers, crushing his skull, and blood began to float about the compartment as they experienced zero G again.

"Secure that!" barked Ikeda, and one man grabbed the crate of explosives, quickly lashing a cargo strap around it. Another pulled the dead man's body armor off and tied his uniform blouse over the crushed head, containing the flow of blood. Then normal gravity returned as they dropped into what the compensators could handle.

"We have particle weapons engaging the hull," said Ichijou, "mask up in case of decompression!" The soldiers did so, but one immediately threw up in his helmet, and he cracked the seal again, struggling not to choke, even as they rolled furiously, to keep the weapons from burning through one spot.

Ichijou had no copilot, and sweat burned her eyes as she wrestled with the unfamiliar controls. She could have asked Ikeda to help her, but he needed to be with his team. Her heads up display traced the normally invisible particle beams, and she thanked the gods that they had expended most of their missiles on the first attack. The three they had sent out at her had caused the violent maneuvering, and this was a shuttle, not a combat vehicle. It handled like a slug, and it was all she could do to keep the belly oriented to the station and keep closing with it. She took a second to glance up at the readout, closing speed two thousand forty eight KPH, intercept thirty seconds.

There was a loud BANG and alarms started to blare, as the particle beams burned through and penetrated the hull. One intersected Sergeant Major Shimada and blew him into a pink mist, the explosion of his superheated body fluids hammering the other soldiers in their hard suits. With a shriek, air started to scream out through the two holes in the ship, as one thruster exploded and sent the ship into a roll. Wallace slapped a patch over one hole, and parts of the Sergeant Major jammed the rest, if only for a moment.

The Empress cut fuel to the damaged engine, yelled "HANG ON!" into the intercom, spun the ship, and lit the main engines. A jet of fire lanced outward from the three nozzles, and the men inside were thrown towards the back ramp. One landed with an audible CRACK as his neck broke.

"GO GO GO!" screamed Ichijou, and she hammered down on the emergency release controls for the back ramp. Explosive bolts blew it outward as they came to a dead stop thirty meters from the station, Earth hanging far below them. *My God*, thought Ikeda as he grabbed a demolition pack and pushed off towards the station, *it's beautiful*.

One man missed his mark and flew up and over the orbital, gabbing frantically at the smooth station skin before heading out into space, his scream of despair echoing through their radios until Ikeda cut it off. The remaining five soldiers, Ikeda, Wallace, one Japanese and two Aussies, clustered around the docking hatch, each emplacing their demolition charge.

Holding on to their magnetic clamps, they set their timers, then leaned back away from the airlock. The original plan had been for the shuttle to mate with the docking collar and go in through atmosphere, but that had gone all to hell on their approach. Speed was of the essence, before the defenders could rally. Behind the second door of the air lock could be a whole platoon of Wolverines, though the Americans had met only token resistance when they had taken theirs. Then again the station had been blown wide open, killing most of the defenders. They HAD to get in before the Invy locked their computers.

As soon as the charges exploded and the debris had spun away, the men crowded into the airlock, and Ichijou spun the shuttle so it was nose on, gently setting the mating collar, even as they worked to set more charges on the inner door. There had to be air pressure in the lock, or they would have explosive decompression of the entire station, and no one knew enough about Invy tech to guarantee they could get the environmental systems running again.

The soldiers crowded back into the shuttle, and opened cases that had protected their rifles from the punishing cold of vacuum as the pilot repressurized the space. With a CRACK that was deafening in the confined space, the charges blew and the inner airlock door sagged backwards.

Wallace ran forward, jammed his P-90 into the open space between the doors, and emptied a full magazine into the area behind, waving it from side to side. They had only basic knowledge of the station from the Americans; their radio had been destroyed before they could send detailed info.

The remaining Japanese soldier grabbed a crowbar and forced the buckled doors apart, and Ikeda threw a stun grenade into the space. It went off with a BANG and a dazzling flash of light, and two men pulled the doors apart as Ikeda and Wallace charged through, rifles up and ready to fire.

Inside was a slaughter house. The bodies of five Wolverines lay on the floor, one still trying to bring his plasma rifle to bear. Wallace shot the creature in the head, and the soldiers moved out, towards the heart of the station. One stayed back to guard the entrance of the shuttle; unless they could capture another docked one, it was their only way back, damaged as it was.

The Japanese soldier, Senior Private Kato, was startled by a movement behind him, and almost shot the figure that emerged from the ship. Captain Ichijou had taken off her helmet and carried her own P-90, on a chest harness. Strapped to her back was her sword.

"Which way did they go, Private?" she asked him.

"Empress, to the left." The station was in the form of a giant wheel, to provide spin if the anti-gravity failed.

"Then we go right," she said, as gunfire echoed, men shouted, Wolverines barked and plasma weapons hiss-cracked.

Chapter 57

The corridor they walked down was eerily deserted, and smelled strongly of fur and scale. Each step that the pilot and the soldier took made the tension grow, until Ichijou's heart was pounding in her chest. This type of combat was far removed from flying a fighter plane at the speed of sound. As if to emphasis the point, SP Kato held up his hand and waved her to fall back behind him. "No offense, Captain, Empress, but you are not trained for this."

Fact was, she knew how to fire the short bullpup rifle, and that was about it. She held a sixth degree *Dan* in Kendo, and would have been far more comfortable wielding the sword that hung at her hip. Its weight felt oddly comforting, but she knew it wouldn't do crap against a plasma rifle.

They came to a doorway that silently slid open as the pair approached, and Kato stepped through, directly into an ambush. The man's reflexes were lightning quick, and he rolled backwards, coming up firing. Ichijou also fired, short bursts at dark figures illuminated by muzzle flash.

The Private yelled, "Fall back!" and she turned, ran backwards several steps, and then spun to provide covering fire for him. Kato emptied his magazine and ran past her, reloading as he ran. In this manner, they withdrew until the corridor turned, and they were no longer in danger of direct fire, but neither stopped running until they found another corridor that turned in towards the center of the station.

"I have tangled with Wolverines before;" he gasped, "and they are fierce, but they cannot shoot for shit!"

At that, they both started laughing hysterically.

***

Ikeda and his men were not having so much luck. One more Australian was dead, and Wallace was slightly wounded. Around a corner was a hasty barricade, with a Dragon hissing at three Wolverines.

"I'll tell you what, mate, I don't think they're happy to see us," said Wallace, through clenched teeth, biting back the pain. Then he leaned over to the corner and yelled, "HEY! DINGOS! SURRENDER AND I'LL GIVE YOU SOME DRAGON STRAIGHT OFF THE BARBIE! TASTES LIKE CHICKEN!"

The response was a hail of plasma that nearly took his head off, chewing away at the corner bulkhead. "I don't think they like chicken," he muttered. Although he appreciated the other mans' humor, Ikeda felt despair inside. They were running out of time.

"I've got an idea," said Peirce, the remaining Aussie Sergeant. With that, he checked his magazine, stood up, and ran out into the corridor, firing and running directly at the barricade. Ikeda was startled, but he also jumped up and followed the soldier, taking time to pick his shots.

Peirce fell as his leg was swept out from under him by a plasma bolt, but he landed with a grunt two thirds of the way down the corridor, and continued to fire. Ikeda jumped over him, screaming at the top of his lungs, and slid like a baseball player into the bottom of the barricade. Carbine empty, he drew his handgun, counted to three, and stood up, arms extended, taking an instant to assess the situation. One Wolverine was down on the ground, howling from a wound, but two were still trading shots with Wallace, who had moved into the corridor. Behind them stood a Dragon, but only carrying a sword.

He engaged the farther one first, lining up the red laser dot on the creature's throat and firing. The Wolverines had very dense bones, and he wasn't sure his 10mm would penetrate a skull. The round punched into the fur, and seemed to have no effect, but he didn't have time to think about it. Two feet to his right, the closer Wolverine turned, ripping claw extended, and Ikeda shot him through the eye. He then turned and fired again at the first one, five shots.

An enormous blow hammered him aside, and the Dragon crashed through the barrier, knocking him down, charging down the corridor at Wallace. Ikeda was too stunned to react as the pistol went flying from his hand, and he watched in horror as the Invy crashed into his friend. Both went down in a tangle of limbs and motion that quickly grew still.

Ikeda ran back down the corridor, passing the still form of Peirce. The Dragon lay dead, and Wallace's arm moved beneath it. With a curse, the Japanese heaved the Invy off the Captain, and knelt by him. The hilt of Wallace's fighting knife stood out from a seam in the Dragon's golden armor, foot long blade sunk deeply. Blood ran from the soldier's mouth, and he coughed as his breath rasped in and out.

Wallace feebly shoved Ikeda's hand away as he tried to see where he was hurt. "Rib's crushed, mate," muttered the Aussie. "No sheilas on the beach for me. Bury me in Oz, brother," he whispered, and his grip fell slack as his breath sighed out and his eyes fixed on the ceiling. The Major pulled the knife out of the Invy's body, and placed it in his friends' bloody hand, closing the fingers around it.

He reloaded his carbine and pistol, took extra ammo off Peirce's body, and shot the wounded Wolverine a half dozen times in the head as the passed through the remains of the barricade.

Chapter 58

Senior Private Kato was fast, but not fast enough. He started to move forward into a large, glass floored room that showed Eastern Asia slowly drifting beneath them. Maybe he was distracted by the sight, or maybe, like Ichijou, he was exhausted. They had killed one more Wolverine in an extended, running gunfight through the halls, ending with Kato taking a deep burn to his neck above his armor. He had also lost his helmet, and both were drenched with sweat.

Maybe that's why he was too slow to see the threat on the other side of the control room. Three Wolverines stood guard on a Dragon who was manipulating a hologram, assisted by two of the octopus creatures. Beyond a large window, a square pallet shape was being maneuvered into place, holding hundreds of titanium rods. Enough to hammer Earth into submission. Kato did shoot, but only got off two rounds before a large caliber plasma beam hit him square in the torso.

All this the Empress saw over his shoulder as she raised her own weapon, but Kato's body slammed her backwards into the corridor. She struggled to push him off, rolling the steaming corpse to the side and staggering to her feet. "Ikeda!" she called over the radio, but there was no answer. "Wallace! Anyone!" No answer. This was it, then, down to her.

She leaned over and blindly fired her remaining cartridges, only a dozen till the weapon clicked dry, and brought her hand back as plasma fired hammered into the corner. Looking down to see if Kato had any, she saw that the plasma bolt had punched a hole in his chest and mangled all his equipment, including his rifle.

Damn. Well, she had heard stories from Ikeda about single combat with Wolverines. There was a legend in the Scouts about a man named Zicavik, Zivcovic or something, who had killed more than one, and the Wolverines respected the results.

Maybe. Maybe she could kill all three, and then the Dragon. Then she realized that she didn't need to kill all of them, only get past them and the Dragon. Seizing the station would be great, but blowing it in place would work too. She reached down into a small pouch on Kato's body, and removed the cool grey cylinder. The antimatter directional mine, if placed against the computer control unit, would be enough to destroy it, according to R&D. Of course, it might depressurize the station too. She estimated her chances to be one in a hundred, and she would die soon after, either from an Invy claw or the explosion itself.

If she was to die, then she was to die. She breathed deeply, oxygenating her body, and unsnapped the rifle from her harness. She threw it outward into the space, and a plasma bolt bisected it. Then, drawing *Kusanagi* from its scabbard, she carefully tested the balance, learning the weight of it, and sending a few practice swings through the air. It felt different from a Kendo pole, and different from the traditional Katana shape, but it also felt like an extension of her arm.

"This is absurd," she whispered. "I'm holding a two thousand year old sword, in a space station, about to fight aliens that look like wolves, and try to kill a six armed Dragon, to plant an antimatter charge, and destroy a semi-intelligent computer. You just can't make this shit up. What next, Cowboy Be-bop comes to my fucking rescue on the space battleship Yamoto?"

Ichijou stopped when she realized she was talking to herself. She could, actually, blow the station from right where she stood, but maybe, just maybe, she could kill all three and gain control. Her fatigue made it hard to make a decision. She looked at the sword to try and feel some mystical connection, but really, it was just an ancient piece of steel and bronze. It would have to do, though, and she could think of no better way for such an heirloom to be used. If a Divine Wind was to save Japan, it would have to be her.

She extended the blade around the corner, waiting for a plasma bolt to knock it from her hand. When it didn't, she extended her arm, and heard excited barks from the Wolverines. Tentatively, she withdrew the sword and then stepped forward, holding it low.

Beneath her feet, the clear glass still showed the edge of the continent, and overlaying that was a targeting matrix. Yellow spots hovered over each of the villages in Japan, with a smattering in Northern China. Central China and Korea, she knew, were radioactive wastelands with no Invy presence.

In front of her stood two of the Wolverines, one wearing the gold bars of a Kuff, or Commander. The other was a Subcommander, and at their feet lay the body of a dead Senior Hashut, or Sergeant. Thank you, Kato, she whispered. The odds were no longer so impossible, just bad. The Dragon ignored her, continuing to remotely maneuver the ammunition pod into place.

She stepped forward, and raised the sword to her face, then assumed a *Kusami no Kamae* position, sword raised high over her shoulder. The Subcommander stepped forward, but his superior growled and shoved him aside, extending his ripping claws.

Careful, she thought to herself, he will not move as a traditional opponent. She advanced slowly, until they both stood almost within striking range of each other. She could smell its sweat matted fur and rotten meat breath, but ignored it and sought the calm place, the place that told her when to strike, watching the creature's eyes for the tell.

They both moved at the same time, a whirlwind of blurring motion, and she felt a claw draw softly along her throat, just breaking her skin. The sword crashed downward, slicing completely though the tough fur of the creatures' own neck, cutting through the jugular.

Never pausing, she spun in place, just as the other Wolverine moved at her. She caught that one with both arms fully extended, blade moving like a whirlwind. The Subcommander's head flew from its shoulders, and she continued, pivoting on the ball of her foot and striking forward at the Dragon.

The Sword of Japan shattered on the alloy armor with a ringing crack and her arms went numb. Ichijou fell to her knees in shock, and the Dragon turned, picked her up, and slammed her to the floor. She felt something crack in her arm, and bones ground together as it picked her up again, hissing with laughter. Again she was slammed to the floor, and her head hit the glass matrix, sending pain rocketing through her and making stars appear.

The six limbed Invy picked her up again, and Ichijou looked downward, to see Japan laid out below her in all its glory, shattered pieces of the sword gleaming in the strange Invy light, mixed with Wolverine blood. She closed her eyes as the creature raised her even higher, and prepared to die. She had done her best, and hoped her ancestors would let her join them. Regret washed over her as she realized she would have no descendants to honor her, though. With her last strength, she struggled to arm the antimatter charge, and smiled one last time as her finger found the cap over the switch, jammed her thumb under it, and pried it off. Then she shoved it forward, and dropped it. Ten minutes till they would be dust in space; she hoped it was in time to stop the strikes.

Major Ikeda fired from thirty meters away, his shaky, blood covered hands steadying for just a second. The 10mm round entered the Dragon's mouth and exited out of the back of its skull, and the creature fell, dropping the Empress to the floor.

Chapter 59

Ikeda said nothing, merely glanced at the flashing light on the antimatter charge, bent down, and picked the stunned pilot off the floor. She screamed as he handled her broken arm and went limp, passing out from the pain. He slung her over his shoulder and started to run, but stopped when he saw the shattered pieces of the sword on the floor. Grunting with effort, for he also was exhausted, the Major reached down, picked up the hilt, which contained about half the length of the sword, and slipped it through a loop on his battle armor.

The scout didn't know how much time they had before the charge blew, or if there were any other Invy on the station, or even how to get back to the shuttle. He just charged blindly forward, trusting to luck and instinct. He was, after all, a Scout, and finding his way was what they were supposed to do.

A turn to the left took him into a blind corridor after a hundred meters, and he cursed, back tracking. Although Ichijou was a woman, she was still fairly heavy in her armor, and unconscious bodies were dead weight. He was sweating profusely in the hotter, humid Invy atmosphere, and there was some element in the air that irritated his lungs.

This wasn't going to work. Ikeda set the pilot down gently on the corridor and propped her up against the wall. He slowly removed her armor, being careful to gently slide it over her arm, wincing. Next, he laid the arm across her chest, and wrapped duct tape around her body, securing it. In the back of his mind, time was screaming at him to MOVE, but he worked as carefully as he could.

Next he unbuttoned his small medical kit. Inside were things that any Special Operations Soldier might need in the field, and he spilled them out on to the floor. Tampons for gunshot wounds, a small precious packet of nanos for blood clotting and antibiotic, tourniquet, rubber bands, three syringes of morphine with auto injectors, and damn, no smelling salts. He sometimes carried them, when he could get them. They were often just the thing to wake you the hell up, which is what he needed his companion to do right now. Then he remembered, and fumbled at another pouch. There, yes, there it was. A small bottle of dried *wagiri togarashi* powder, Japanese red pepper, which he used to flavor his bland MRE's. Good for throwing Wolverines off the track, too.

Ikeda opened the bottle and poured a bit into the palm of his hand, spit on it, mixing it into a paste. Then he took a small amount and wiped it just under her nose, conscious of time passing. "Forgive me, Kiyomi," he said, then placed his hand over her mouth and gently blew on her nose. Reflexively, her nostrils flared, and the scent of the wagari wafted into her sinuses. Her eyes flew open, and she sneezed powerfully, then tried to stand up. Ikeda grabbed her by her good arm, and lifted her to her feet. "RUN!" he yelled in her ear, and they did, fleeing down the corridor.

They had gone only twenty meters when the Empress grabbed his arm and dragged him back to a doorway that led to another corridor, one he wouldn't have taken. The pair made a turn, and Ikeda recognized the corridor his team had first advanced down, only minutes ago; it seemed like a lifetime. The shuttle airlock was ahead on their right, and he almost shoved Ichijou forward, feeling time running out.

They were ten meters from the hatch when the gravity went out, probably in response to the antimatter charge detonating, and alarms began to blare. Ikeda stumbled forward, flew head over heels, and continued to spin, instantly disoriented. Ichijou, though, was in her element, reaching her good arm out to grab a handle set in the airlock door, and hooking her legs out towards the Major as he flew past. She screamed with agony as her bad arm banged against the door, and almost passed out again. With a supreme force of will, she managed to hold on as Ikeda grabbed at her leg; he may have been weightless, but he still had mass and momentum.

Breathing heavily, she fought the pain as he pulled himself up her body and then grabbed the handle himself. Together, they swung into the airlock and he helped her transition to the shuttle's artificial gravity, gently setting her down on the floor. Thankfully the cabin that lead to the nose mounted airlock was pressurized, but there was a short ladder to climb. He helped her up again, and slowly, they got up into the cabin.

Outside the front viewport, the station was slowly breaking up. "Kiyomi," he said, forgetting in his urgency who he was talking to and using her first name, "I can pilot this thing, but I need you to tell me what to do."

She motioned weakly to a large red handle, and he pulled it, just as something exploded silently in the central area of the station. Fragments pinged off the hull as the docking clamps were released. The shuttle sat there for a moment until Ikeda realized that he needed to back away. The engine controls were similar to the ones on the transport he had commandeered, enough so that he could slowly send them backwards. Then he tried to turn, and went into a wild spin as the damaged thruster started firing erratically.

An exhausted Ichijou dragged herself into the copilots' seat, which was uncomfortable to her, made for a Dragon. She slapped some controls, and took the stick in her good hand, fighting the centrifugal force that was trying to throw her around the cockpit, too quickly for the inertial dampeners to respond.

Eventually, the spinning stopped, and they sped away from the slowly disintegrating space platform. Ichijou aimed them into a low earth orbit, and opened a radio channel to the Americans in the other station. She knew that they were proceeding in the opposite orbit, and would come around the horizon soon.

"That was stupid," Ikeda said as he helped her down to the cockpit floor.

She bristled at that, and said, "Excuse me?"

"Fighting as a soldier, going into the station. I had it under control."

"You forget yourself, MAJOR!" she said, anger rising in her voice. "I am the EMPRESS OF JAPAN!"

"Yes," he answered, "and you put yourself needlessly at risk."

She was truly mad now, and spat back, "What I do or don't do is none of your concern, MAJOR Ikeda!"

"As Major Ikeda, no, it is not my concern, and I honor your bravery. As a man who has loved, and lost, it concerns me greatly. I do not want to lose again." And he leaned forward, kissing her gently on the lips. Then he sat back, closed his eyes, and fell fast asleep.

Captain Kiyomi Ichijou looked at him in amazement, and started to laugh. A deep, long laugh that, despite her arm, felt amazingly good. In the last eight hours, she had seen a nuclear weapon go off, shot down four enemy interceptors, ejected from a disintegrating aircraft, spent an hour floating on a raft, been rescued, fought a space battle, engaged in gunfights, had a sword battle with aliens, and played Ultimate Fighting Champion with a six armed lizard.

Maybe falling in love wasn't a bad way to end the day.

Part IV

"The Blood of Tyrants"

Outside the ruins of Olympia, Washington

"For Christ's sake men—come on! Do you want to live forever?"
~ Sergeant Major Daniel Joseph "Dan" Daly, France, 1917

Chapter 60

Though there were electric street lights in the Invy towns, and some businesses were linked to the fusion reactor, the houses were forbidden power. Instead, oil lamps burned dully; and few were lit at this hour. Not even the pre-dawn glow lit the eastern sky, still in the dead of night, and Mount Rainier blocked out the stars.

In the basement of a house, close to the edge of the small town, a man grunted as he heaved at a paving stone. He wasn't as young as he had been when the Invy came and his unit dispersed from Fort Lewis, eleven years ago. In the intervening time, until he had come to live in this damned place, he and his family had often starved, and he still wore the scars of heavy fighting against refugees. Some were on his skin, and others were in his soul.

The stone came up, and he moved it aside. Underneath, a set of wooden steps descended into the darkness, and a damp smell wafted up at him. The lamp guttered as he carried it downward and hung it on a peg, the yellow glow illuminating dark green cases with stenciled markings.

Half an hour later, he had carried all the boxes up into the basement, and set about opening them. First, the rifle case, hissing as he equalized the air pressure, to reveal an M-6 carbine, a dozen empty magazines, and a cleaning kit. He set about breaking down the weapons, inspecting each piece, and gently oiling them, then snapped everything back in place.

Another case yielded an optical sight, powered by the movement of the weapon in his hands. Shaking it up and down several times, the red dot appeared, and he snapped it onto the rail mount. The same for a PVS-48 night vision headset, the screen slaved to the aiming sight on his rifle, the true color display bright in the lamplight, readings for the 25mm grenade launcher flashing red, closer than the minimum arming distance.

He fed 6mm sabot rounds into the magazines, forty each, designed to penetrate Wolverine armor. They had been smuggled in five years ago from Cascades base, and he said a silent prayer that they worked. His own body armor still fit; not much chance of putting on weight with the meager Invy rations. Heavy layers designed to dissipate plasma energy overlapped each other in an articulated, insect like covering.

Before he put on the armor, though, one last detail. He shrugged out of the heavy, rough trader's clothes he wore, and pulled on the grey, green, brown and black mottled uniform that had lain folded in another container. Before shrugging into the blouse, he looked at the subdued CEF patch on the shoulder, and beneath that the tan and black American flag. He ripped them off the Velcro and swapped, so that the Stars and Stripes rode above the Sunburst and Globe. Last, he rubbed the three stripes and two rockers of his sewn on rank, his nametape, BLAKE, and his Combat Infantry Badge, for luck.

"Dad? What are you doing?" Blake jumped, startled at the sound of his teenaged son's voice. The boy stood at the head of the stairs, looking down at the collection of opened cases.

"Alex, go back upstairs," his father told him, but his son descended the steps. He was fifteen, and had spent the last eight years living and learning at the Invy School in town. His father had tried to counteract their propaganda, but as the boy had grown older and entered his teens, their arguments had grown with him.

"Dad, what is all this?" Time to come clean, his father knew, and he sighed inwardly.

The man stood up and motioned his son down into the basement, sitting down on a chair as he cradled his rifle. "Alex, do you remember what I did, before the war?"

The boy shook his head, staring in mute wonder at the gear. "You were a truck driver. I remember you being gone on long trips."

"No. I was a soldier, Alex. Special Operations, Confederated Earth Forces. Before that, 75th Ranger Regiment, US Army."

"Did you … did you fight in the war?" asked his son, bewilderment on his face. He had been only four when the orbital strikes had thundered down, and remembered none of it.

"I did, as much as anyone did. Tried to maintain law and order after the strikes, then we fought when the Invy came, until we broke."

"But Dad, they're our friends! They came to save the Earth from environmental damage. We were destroying our planet!"

Eric Blake sighed and said, "That's what they tell you in school. We've had this argument a thousand times, Alex. They're here to make us their slaves."

"That's not true, and you know it," said the teen passionately. "And what is all this?" He gestured to the weapons and equipment.

"It's time, is what it is. Time to do something. I want you to stay here; things are going to be pretty hot over the next day. If we lose, take some of this gear into the mountains, where we have our camp. There's plenty of supplies there. Eventually, I suppose, the Invy will let you come back, or I'll come for you."

His son took a step back up the stairs, a look of horror on his face. "What do you mean, we?"

"The CEF, son. Last roll of the dice, I suppose," answered his father in a weary tone.

"I … I can't let you do that!" said his son, and he turned and fled up the stairs.

"ALEX! WAIT!" shouted his father, running after him, up the stairs and into the darkness. The sergeant was supposed to meet up with his team in a few minutes; there was no time for this.

He had just caught up with him, rounding a corner, when both almost crashed into a Wolverine patrol that was passing down their street, two of the creatures walking side by side. They caught sight of Blake with his rifle, strictly forbidden, just as Alex yelled to them. Both instantly lowered their plasma rifles off their shoulders and flicked off the safeties.

Erik Blake, veteran of Afghanistan, the Spratly War, and the disastrous invasion, took the chanciest shot in his life. The rifle rose, aim and trigger pull were as one, and the bullet scored his son's shoulder, then caught the closest Wolverine, just as the Invy soldier raised its own weapon. Blood, black in the street light, splattered, and Alex Blake screamed in pain, dropping to his knees.

The second Wolverine looked at its dead comrade, howled a challenge and rushed at the soldier with incredible speed, dropping its rifle and raising its arms. Blake leapt over his prone son and crashed into his sworn enemy, digging his fingers into the things' throat, even as fangs reached for his own. He used his weight to bear the smaller creature to the ground, sharp teeth burying themselves into his arm and clamping down, trying to puncture through his tough uniform. The Wolverine, incredibly strong, forced him back upwards until they stood together in the street in a macabre death dance. He felt ripping claws slicing at his armor, seeking a joint to penetrate, and began to weaken.

Suddenly the creature's head snapped back, hammered through the side of its skull by a heavy 7.62 bullet, and it fell backwards into the dust. Blake stood, chest heaving with exertion and shaking with adrenaline, as the rest of ODA 352 rushed down the side of the street. He grabbed his son, lifting him up, ignoring his scream of pain, and shoved him back towards the door of his house. "Get inside, and stay there, no matter what happens!" he yelled at his son, and the boy, thoroughly frightened, blood streaming down his arm, nodded once and fled.

Major Cliff knelt, ignoring the scene behind her, watching to see if there was any activity at the Invy government buildings. Blake knelt down beside her, seating his NVG's and taking up his sector.

"Are we ready?" she asked, and the veteran NCO took a deep breath to calm himself.

"Let's do this, Ma'am."

She glanced at him, nodded, said, "Follow me."

"Rangers lead the way!" he shot back reflexively, making her eyes roll, and they moved out into the darkness, more than a dozen men and women wearing the patches of the CEF and the United States.

Chapter 61

The Invy compound lay across a cleared field of fire, a hundred meters from the first houses of the town, with the Greens militia barracks forming a T behind it. The team gathered in the darkness around a corner for a quick review of the plan.

The ODA had spent eight years living in the town, planning, waiting for this day, trying to counter the propaganda being taught at the Invy school. It had been hard, though, because the majority of the town dwellers had all the fight beaten out of them by defeat and starvation, trading freedom for security. Blake couldn't even really blame them, but it didn't make what they were about to do any easier.

"OK," said Major Cliff, "let's go over the plan one more time."

Each member of the team had a specific job to do, from weapons crews to several who were to go from house to house, spreading the word. There were five thousand people in the town; over the years they had carefully felt out who would or wouldn't support them. It numbered around a hundred, mostly veterans.

"Alpha, you're taking out the APC. Bravo," Major Cliff said, "you have the MK-19. It's your job to nail the Invy infantry as they come out the gate. Charlie, you've got the Green's barracks, but first set up the MG for an enfilade of the gate. We're going to need a serious base of fire to pin them down while we rally support." Master Sergeant Cordell would be in charge of that team, and he had a few surprises of his own for them. The wiry black man nodded; this was his specialty.

"Alpha, as soon as the APC is down, I need you to fall back on me so we can assault into the compound, once reinforcements get here." SFC Lynch nodded; he and his team knew the compound in detail, and had complete confidence they could take the Invy in CQB.

"Delta, Echo, house to house of our supporters. Assembly at the warehouse for weapons distribution. Form them into squads and send them back here." The two team leaders, Lieutenant Sanchez and SSG Chu, looked at each other. This had been their part of the plan to create, and the two women had been instrumental in identifying the right people.

"Let's do this, Cholo," said Chu.

Sanchez slapped her gloved hand and answered, "In your face, China doll!" The two gathered their men and hustled off into the darkness, avoiding the streetlights.

"Foxtrot, you've got killing to do. Get to it."

Blake started to speak, but the Major cut him off. "Couldn't be helped, Erik. Get to work. I want all those bastard Green traitors dead. To work, people." She looked at her watch, and continued, "We've now got four minutes, based on the average reaction time of the Invy at this time of night. They'll come out looking for their two missing. I want the ambush set up right as their gate opens."

The most savage of conflicts is always a civil war, with no quarter given. Erik Blake knew what he and his two companions were about to do, and didn't like it; but he understood the necessity. He just hoped there was no collateral damage. "Fat fucking chance," he muttered.

Fortunately for them, the humans who had decided to actively work with the Invy, not just go along to get along, all lived in a cluster of houses close by the Invy compound. It took the three men less than a minute to jog to their first target, the captain of the Green Militia.

"You know," whispered Sergeant Sotelo, "I really wish we didn't get this job."

Blake answered, "Just focus on the mission, Tomas."

"Yeah, but his kids are going to be scarred for life," said his partner, SSG Carballo.

"No shit, but it's better than slavery, which is where it's all going to end. Now focus," Blake told his subordinates, "we've got five minutes for the first three targets. After that, we just go to work on the list, get as many as we can, and then join the real fight."

They had made their way to the fence around the back door off the house, and Carballo, who was tallest, peeked over. Thank God the Invy hated dogs; the former gangbanger could only imagine what this would have been like in his old neighborhood of Tacoma. Half a dozen starving pit bulls waiting to tear your ass up.

"Clear!" he whispered, and then boosted Sotelo over the fence. Blake was next, then Carballo handed over his rifle and vaulted it. They gathered at the back door, each thinking of the layout of the house. They had all, for one reason or another, found a reason to visit the Green Commander. It was the same exact layout as the house next door, the Mayors.

Blake reached over and slowly turned the doorknob. Like all houses in Invy towns, it was required to remain unlocked, to allow searches by any Invy, at any time. He slowly pushed the door open, and the three men filed inside, weapons scanning the kitchen, night vision eliminating the darkness. Each had slung their rifle in exchange for a suppressed 10mm handgun, and their infrared aiming lasers tracked across the walls.

"OK, let's go!" said Blake, and they charged through the house and up the stairs. Without gunshots, people next door would just as soon mind their own business this late at night. Carballo stayed behind to watch the front door, Blake and Sotelo leading with their pistols. Sotelo went right at the top of the stairs, to block any threat from the hallway. Blake turned left, and kicked in the bedroom door with his boot.

Captain Denning was lying half on and half off the bed, eyes open to eternity, pistol lying by his outstretched hand, his throat still oozing out drips of blood. His wife, Catherine, stood over him, blood on her nightgown, knife in hand. Blake froze, unable to process what he was seeing.

"We heard you come in the back door. It's tonight, isn't it?" she said.

Blake answered flatly, "Yes," and lowered his pistol.

"Good. Kill them all."

The NCO kicked the pistol away from her reach, and said simply, "Stay here, protect your kids. It may get pretty bad."

She nodded and sat down on her bed, looking at the body of her husband. Then she spit on the corpse.

Blake turned and called to Sotelo, and the two went down the stairs at a run, joined by Carballo. The three went out the back door again, and headed next door.

"What happened?" asked Carballo as they repeated the fence climbing into the Mayor's yard.

"Wife smoked him," answered Blake, as he approached the back door.

Sotelo whispered, "Rough night in the hood, esse!"

The three men entered the Mayors house, and again, stormed up the stairs, or started to. At the top, in the darkness, a form moved, showing the Mayor, a fat man in a world of starvation, just exiting the bathroom. The two Special Forces soldiers fired at the same time, their pistols making several barking coughs each; the man fell backwards against the wall, blood streaks showing red on the white paint. His corpulent body started sliding down the stairs at them, but they had already turned, racing for their next target.

Chapter 62

"Is this going to work?"

Cliff looked at her NCOIC, grinning broadly in the darkness. "Well, it's not what we had planned, but the missing Wolverines will just add to it. You ready, Carl?"

"I've been ready for eleven years, Lauren. Is it time?" said the Master Sergeant.

Lauren Cliff looked at her watch, counting down to H-Hour, even as the Confederated Earth Forces set into motion. Five thousand miles to the west, the first of the surface to space missiles broached the Pacific Ocean, and Captain Kiyomi Ichijou slammed backwards in her seat as her F-22 broke the speed of sound. A thousand miles to the East, David Warren prepared to fight a war a million miles away. Three thousand miles further, Scout Team One took out a patrol on a runway, and Master Sergeant Nick Agostine started to run. On the other side of the world, Private Tommy Atkins fired his .50 caliber, the stock of the rifle slamming into his shoulder.

She knew nothing of the actions of the rest of the CEF around the world; the ODA team leader was only concerned with her small part of it. Still, she could feel the tension of the men and women around her. Five soldiers who knew that they might not, probably wouldn't, live to see the end of this, and that they were a part of much bigger things. But, she thought, at least we'll see the beginning.

"I just want to tell you all, you're the best people I've ever known," she said out loud, "Four, three, two…"

At 'one', there was a flash of light, followed by a muffled CRUMP as the power lines from the antimatter reactor to the town were blown. There were no words said, no motivational "hooah's", just professionals going to work.

The machine gun team hustled to the right, moving to a position to enfilade the front gate, while three men moved left, around the block, working feverishly to set up the tripod mounted heavy plasma cannon, just around the corner on the main road leading out toward the power plant. Their job was to trip the ambush by firing point blank into the APC, and assaulting forward to kill any Wolverine survivors. Then they would move to complete the cross fire on the killing ground.

When the gate opened, and the APC had turned left and moved out, an MK-19 automatic grenade launcher would be maneuvered to fire right back into the compound. Sergeant Sean Dodson cradled the eighty pound weapon in his arms, leaning back against the brick wall, heart racing with anticipation. Beside him, SSG Rob Booth had the tripod resting over his shoulder, and two boxes of grenades at his feet as he knelt on the cracked pavement. "You ready, Sean?" asked the Staff Sergeant.

Dodson patted the heavy weapon, and whispered the grenadier's motto, "Because fuck you, and fuck you, and fuck everyone around you!" His shotgun was leaning up against the wall, safety on but within easy reach. He had fought Wolverines before.

The gate opened; no slack on the Invy reaction time. The APC moved out, kicking up a cloud of dust, obscuring the dozen troops assembling in the court yard for a foot patrol. Swiveling on its fans, the tank sized vehicle turned and headed southward, disappearing around the building to the left.

Everything seemed to slow down for Dodson and Booth. Their fellow soldiers faded into the background as they executed the maneuver they had practiced a hundred times. Although Booth was a higher rank, he knew Dodson had the weight to handle the big gun easily, and was content to feed him and call corrections.

He opened the tripod and pushed it out around the corner, even as Dodson swung the launcher down, seated it home, and flipped open the feed tray. A belt of grenades was slapped in, and the gunner sat down on the ground, weapon between his legs, racking the slide back. He took a second to check his aim; the distance had already been carefully measured out.

One breath later, he heard and felt the SIZZLE CRACK of the plasma cannon, and all the hair on his arms stood up, even two blocks away. Pulling the trigger, he watched as the first three rounds left the tube, and kicked it slightly right even as they detonated. THUMP THUMP THUMP was felt more than heard.

The antimatter containment unit on the APC let go in a thunderous roar that shattered every window around them, showering them with glass, but neither Dodson nor Booth deviated from their task, walking the grenades in a continuous stream into the charging Wolverines.

"I don't think that was supposed to happen!" grunted the gunner, heaving the weapon around. A half dozen of the Invy troops spilled from the gate, and beside the grenade team Corporal Raj Havner let fly with his sniper rifle, working the bolt furiously. From the side, the machine gun team started cutting them down with enfilading fire, but the aliens moved too quickly for the gun to follow them.

Behind the three men, Major Cliff shouldered her own rifle and placed the red dot sight on the closest creature, breathed out, and fired. Discarding the sabot, a three millimeter depleted uranium dart hammered into the chest armor of the Wolverine, knocking it backwards.

One stopped to turn and engage the machine gun team, while three more charged forward, firing their plasma rifles on automatic from the hip. One bolt hit Havner in the head, exploding with a CRACK and sending a cloud of superheated blood and brains over the grenadiers, who had shifted their fire into the windows of the Greens barracks.

Cliff fired again, missed, trying to hold steady in the face of the incoming fire, breathing violently as adrenaline coursed through her. It had been a decade since she had been able to properly train, and she cursed at herself to settle down. "Come on, you bastards!" she yelled, firing and missing as her target swerved from side to side, moving incredibly fast. Her next shot took the leg off one, but the other two were almost on them.

She screamed as a plasma bolt hammered into her own armor, and it started to burn as she struggled to unlatch it and pull it off. The first Wolverine to reach them dropped his rifle in its sling and extended a ripping claw, stabbing downward into Booths' back; the soldier had ignored the Wolverine and continued to feed the grenade launcher, caught up in his job. He screamed loudly as the claw ripped through him and drove into the concrete, then pulled back out. The wounded soldier grabbed the alien around its legs and rolled over on top of it, struggling furiously.

A shout from behind her as the second one crashed into the ODA leader, slashing furiously at her, even as she slipped her arms out of the superheated armor. She fell to the concrete, smashing her face as the ripping claw glanced off her helmet. The return stroke slashed across her leg, even as a shotgun boomed. She felt the creature knocked off her, and struggled to her feet, drew her pistol, and fired half the magazine into the one stabbing at Booth. It was knocked backwards, and fell to the ground twitching. The Staff Sergeant lay still, a half a dozen stab wounds draining his life out onto the ground. Dodson sat back down behind the grenade launcher, reached over the body of his friend, and fed in another belt, hammering the Green barracks.

Chapter 63

Johanna Sanchez had lived for this moment. All the cat calls, the muttered word "whore" under women's breaths, spending nights with men she despised. All that was coming to a head.

"Hey, Chu," she laughed as they approached the first house, "it's all coming to a head! Get it?"

"Yeah," said the fifth generation Asian American, "I get it. Way too much, cholo." Even before the war, she had endured her own tormentors, and when ODA 352 had been assigned to this town, it had gotten worse. Both she and Sanchez had been outsiders in this mostly white community, but for a while, refugees hadn't cared. When things had settled down, and some had begun to become fat and happy under Invy rule, the subtle discrimination had started again. Maybe it would have been different, but by their own planning, Staff Sergeant Chu and Lieutenant Sanchez had become, for all intents and purposes, the town whores.

What it had allowed them to do was develop actionable intelligence, granting them access to floor plans of houses, and even get escorted through the Invy buildings. Along the way they had identified those who held hatred of the Invy, all military veterans. Most were just trying to survive, but some had indicated they would fight, if only someone would organize it. They had said nothing, but made careful note. A week before, ten of them had been brought, individually, to a deserted warehouse by other team members and been told to each reach out to a list of ten more, to be ready for action. The following days had been tense, and one had sought to gain favor with the Invy by going to the Greenies. He had never gotten there, courtesy of a knife in the kidney by Chu while she was in bed with him, after he told her his intentions.

They and their two other soldiers split up, going to opposite doors on the street, and, when they opened to hammering fists, told the men who answered one word. "FREEDOM!" they each said, and hurried down the street. Behind them, the doors closed, and then quickly opened again, the notified men hurrying out into the night. They had just reached the ninth house when the night erupted with a CRUMP, the explosion taking down the power lines, and the street went dark.

"Good enough!" said Sanchez, and they both broke into a dead run to their safe house. Charging through the unlocked door, followed by Sergeants Jimmie Patton and Dave "Doc" Cofer. The four of them pushed hard at a wall, and it rotated slightly on well-oiled hinges to reveal a narrow room, perhaps four feet wide. Enough room for the olive drab military hardware cases lined up in rows. They started breaking them out as gunfire echoed up and down the village, and the first volunteers showed up a minute later, staring at the four in their CEF uniforms. Sanchez stood on top of one box as even more showed up, and held up her arms for quiet, just as the antimatter containment bottle let go on the APC.

"Listen up! My name is Lieutenant Johanna Sanchez, Confederated Earth Forces, Special Operations Detachment A 352. The time has come, and we're striking back all over the world."

They all stared at her in amazement. For the last decade, almost, they had known her as a high priced prostitute. Hell, some of them had even had her themselves. This was a little much.

"Dave," said one, talking to Sergeant Cofer, who was his neighbor, "what is all this about?"

"Like the LT says, Joe. It's time to hit back."

"And y'all ..."

"We don't have time for this," interrupted Sanchez. "Do you hear that gun and plasma fire? If we don't beat them tonight, what do you think is going to happen? They're going to flatten this town, and everyone in it."

"What about the orbitals?" asked an older man.

"We're hitting them tonight. Don't ask me, I don't know the details. We're only concerned with here and now. Captain Ellison, isn't it?"

"You know damn well it is, Johanna," he grinned, thinking of a few nights her had had with her. She gave him a wink and carried on.

"You're in charge of the town militia, now, Sir. Major Cliff has overall command. We need to get our shit together and hit those Invy bastards. It's do or die time, gentlemen. You're all restored to your last rank, get an armband and sort your shit out. You have five minutes, and then we're moving out to hit the Green Militia Barracks." She jumped down and started opening cases. The rest of the Special Operations team joined her, handing out M-6 carbines. Each was accompanied by a bandolier of pre-packaged forty round magazines, and a blue arm band with the CEF flag under the American flag.

The explosions and gunfire continued, and they worked feverishly. When several dozen men had received weapons, she had them count off by numbers, forming three squads. The veterans quickly fell in, remembering their training and fueled by hatred, each led by one of the CEF operators.

"OK, Captain Ellison, can you stay here, Sir, and organize the rest of the men into a Quick Reaction Force?" She handed him a squad radio, and turned it on. "There's anti-armor weapons in there, we're going to need an ambush on I-5 by Nisqually. There's no ODA between here and there, and the Dragons will be screaming for help. Expect a relief column of several vehicles, possible air cover too."

"Can do, LT. It's great to be back in the saddle again. Take care, and kick their ass!"

"I'm all outta bubble gum, Sir!" said Sanchez with a grin, saluted, and motioned to each of the Sergeants leading a squad. "Alright, let's move out! First squad on point, second follow, third set up a blocking position against anyone who might be coming to help the Greens. If they're adults, kill them. If they're kids, Taser 'em."

They headed out into the darkness, lit by flashes of plasma from behind the village buildings. It was time to kill, and time to die.

Chapter 65

Like the maxim says, no plan survives contact with the enemy. Major Cliff sat with her back against the wall, pinned down by accurate plasma fire from inside the compound. Next to her, his leg peppered with shrapnel when a plasma bolt has destroyed the MK-19, sat Sergeant Dodson. There weren't enough Invy alive now to take the fight to them, and no one ever said they were stupid. The Dragons were probably hunkered down waiting for an orbital strike, screw their troops.

"Alpha," she called again over the team radio. "SITREP, over." No answer. She suspected that they had been taken out when the antimatter containment blew.

"Delta, this is command," she called, "we're going to need the mortars."

"Roger that, we have two 60's with us, and I've got about a dozen rounds HE. Be there in two mikes."

That was good. The mortars, dropped into the compound, would keep the Invy's heads down while they assaulted the gate. That damn gate, though, was a killing funnel, and the walls were too thick to breech. The militia would provide covering fire, but she wasn't going to ask them to go into that funnel.

"Foxtrot, this is command, rally back. Alpha is down, need you here."

"On our way!" came back Blake's voice on the radio, and she breathed a sigh of relief. Good man.

Erik Blake paused at the sixth door he was about to open, one of the most ardent teachers who worked for the Invy. He was breathing heavily; the last house they had assaulted, one of the Green platoon sergeants, had descended into a full blown firefight. The traitor had, unsurprisingly, an "illegal" AK-74 with a ton of ammo, and he had hosed down the team as they had come through the door. The man had probably been alerted by the explosions outside, and was waiting for them. They had backed off, miraculously unhurt, and tried an entry again. That time, Carballo had taken a glancing round off his helmet, so Blake ordered them to pull back out.

"MILLER!" Blake had yelled through the open doorway, "come out or we'll burn the house down! Think about your wife and kids!" The answer was another full magazine blowing through the walls on either side of the doorway.

Blake had told Sotelo to throw a smoke grenade through an upper floor window, and, as the red cloud billowed out, a woman and children could be heard screaming. Miller came charging down the stairs, weapon up at his shoulder, and Carballo had put three rounds into him.

Now, with the firefight raging at the Invy compound, each house was going to be more and more dangerous to go into. Better a straight up battle against the Invy, instead of possibly killing women and children. They could always hang the teacher.

Little needed to be said to his two team mates; just a standard gesture that meant Return To Base; both had heard the conversation over the now active team radios, and the ongoing conversation as Cliff directed two squads to her position. It was weird to be using radio again, and Blake felt an unnatural itch between his shoulders, waiting for the thunderbolt to drop from space. Not that he would know it.

They moved cautiously through the streets, since people were awake now. Seeing their guns and uniforms, some actually cheered from their doorways, and the team made gestures for them to get back inside. Two blocks south of Cliff's position, they came upon two Greens who stumbled out of a house. No doubt they were AWOL from the barracks, teenagers, really, not much older than his son, out hooking up with some girls. They stepped out with their backs to the three Special Operations soldiers, rifles held in their hands as they stared at the flashes of plasma and gunfire.

Sotelo gave Blake a questioning look, and in answer, he lifted his rifle and fired, a two round burst into each. Both men went down, and, as the team rushed past, Blake put a round into the militiamen's heads. A mercy, really. If they were still alive after the 3mm penetrators had run through them, there was no medical facilities to handle their wounds.

"Foxtrot coming in!" called Blake over the radio, and waved his arm around the corner of the building. No need to get shot by his own troops.

"Come up!" came the answer from Cliff. The three men advanced around the corner, to see a dozen men lined up on the side of the building. Each wore an older pair of night vision devices, and were wearing civilian clothes. Even as he came up, three men, led by Sergeant Cofer, ran back to get a clear angle of fire for the mortar they carried, without exposing them to plasma fire.

Blake took a knee next to Cliff. "What's the plan, Ma'am?" he asked, trying to catch his breath. He wasn't twenty anymore. None of them were.

"Mortars are going to lay suppressive fire into the courtyard. Me, Patton, and you three are going to loop around, get under the wall, and charge through the gate, while Dodson directs these guys to lay a base of fire. Between them and the mortars, it should give us breathing room to take the courtyard."

The SFC nodded. He honestly didn't expect to live the night out, and he pushed thoughts of his son far back in his mind. Like someone once said, the way you get through the hell of combat is to realize that you were already dead.

"OK, let's do this then," she said, and stood, knees popping with the effort and the added weight of the armor.

"Did you forget to bring your walker?" asked Blake as they jogged back down the street.

She laughed and said, "Bite me, you ain't so young yourself."

"I was just thinking that," he answered.

In their arrogance, the Invy hadn't erected any watch towers, instead relying on cameras and other sensors to provide surveillance. Master Sergeant Cordell had, in his guise of a worker, disconnected them from their battery backup the night before, so they were clear to approach the only gate from the side.

"You know, in some ways," said Sotelo, "these guys are pretty damn stupid. Makes you wonder how they even beat us."

"Who the hell knows? We can be pretty arrogant ourselves, you know. Bunch 'a towel heads fought us to a stalemate in Afghanistan for thirty years."

"You can't say that!"

"What?" asked Carballo.

"Towelhead," answered his partner.

"Hey, I got mad respect for those towelheads. Wish I had some here to help us now."

Cliff held up her hand to silence them, and they crept slowly up to the gate. The plasma bolts had stopped firing, with no targets in sight. Behind them, the machine gun continued to hammer away at the Green barracks.

"Execute!" called Cliff over the radio, and they heard the THUNK THUNK of the mortars being fired. Each soldier tensed, hoping none of the rounds landed short of the wall. Even before they hit, two more were in the air, then the launches were covered by the almost simultaneous CRACK CRACK of the rounds detonating. When that happened, the militia squad rolled out from behind the corner, and began to lay down a blistering barrage at one side of the twenty foot wide gate.

The last mortar rounds detonated, and Cliff yelled, "GO!" She rolled around the edge of the wall, out into the court yard, laser sight slaved to her NVGs. The beam danced through the dust as she ran into hell.

Chapter 68

The sound of the mortars let Team Charlie know that things were reaching a head. The team leader grabbed the voice amplifier he had slung at his hip, and told his gunner to cease firing.

"GREEN MILITIA!" he called, voice booming out, "THIS IS MASTER SERGEANT CORDELL, CONFEDERATED EARTH FORCES SPECIAL OPERATIONS! THROW YOUR WEAPONS OUT THE WINDOWS AND WE WILL LET YOU GO!" Honestly, as professional as he was, Cordell didn't like killing, especially his fellow human beings. With their leadership taken out by Blake and his team, they really were just a bunch of young men who, under other circumstances, might have been his own soldiers. Might as well give them the chance. The answer was a smattering of shots that came nowhere near his position. Cordell didn't have to give any orders to his machine gunner, who opened back up on the building.

"All I'm saying," yelled Sergeant Eddie Wood, over the hammering of another three round burst into a ground floor window of the barracks, "is that the alien invasion bullshit is just that!" His loader ignored him as she flipped open another can of ammo and joined up the belt, concentrating at the task at hand.

"What do you think, Master Sergeant?" asked Wood, then tapped out another burst at a silhouette in a window that raised a rifle to fire.

"I think," said Master Sergeant Cordell, "that you should shut the hell up and do your job." He paused to listen to the team radio, and then removed a grenade from his vest, slipping it into the launcher under his rifle.

"No more screwing around, Eddie. Watch that doorway, and be ready to nail whoever comes out. Tanchack, you just feed that gun and don't listen to his bullshit."

"Never do, big Sarge, never do," she answered, and grinned at her gunner.

Cordell knew the exact distance from their firing position to the barracks front door. He had welded shut the rear door, hardly ever used, the day before. Sometimes being ignored is almost better than being invisible.

TONK. The black shape arched out and flew through a window in the second floor, and a few seconds later, bright, dazzling light erupted as the Willie Pete splashed out, followed by billowing smoke from the wooden floor catching fire. There were already dozens of bullet holes in the stone façade, and a dozen bodies lay on the ground in front of the door, caught in the first rush.

There were a hundred things that Cordell would have done differently if he had designed the structure, including multiple entrances, bunkers, a direct connection to the Invy compound. Thing was, the Green weren't real soldiers; they were thugs and bullies that the Invy used to keep the population in check. They reminded Cordell of some of the African militias he had fought it the long proxy war with China, before the Invasion. Before his home in Detroit had become a big hole in the ground, mixed with the ashes of his wife and kids.

"GIT SOME!" yelled Sergeant Jessica Tanchack, letting the belt feed through her hands. She wasn't a bloodthirsty person, but she had suffered plenty of abuse at the hands of the Green militia; just about every woman in town had. That, and, well, there was something about being in the middle of a fight and killing your enemy that just made a person's blood boil. The big gun hammered out its song, a tongue of flame racing outwards. When they had engaged the Invy at the gate that had been one thing, like shooting pop up targets of strange shapes, but this was, well, magnificent, and she felt both horrible and ecstatic at the same time as the bodies fell.

Cordell tapped on Woods' leg, and the NCO stopped firing. There was a reason the machine gun had changed war forever at the beginning of the last century; it was very good at what it did, slaughtering your enemy. Not that the men who finally came running out of the burning building were the enemy anymore. The team let them stumble into the night, defeated. If they were smart, they would leave town. If they weren't, well, civil wars are the ugliest of wars, and it would be the rope for most of them.

Even as they ran, Lt. Sanchez arrived with a squad of CEF militia. Although she was, technically, a higher rank than Cordell, he had a dozen more years more experience than she did, and she knew it.

"Jimmy," she said to her squad leader, "search the barracks with these guys. Gather every weapon you can, and see if you can get into their armory before the whole place burns down."

"You got it, Ma'am," he answered, and led the men in through the machine gun pocked front door, directly into the burning building.

"Command, this is Charlie," called Cordell over the radio. He had lost track of what was happening at the Invy compound, knowing that Major Cliff and Team Foxtrot were going in to secure it.

"Charlie, this is Foxtrot. Command is down, and we need some help cracking these doors. We're going to need something that goes bang, really loud."

"I've got what you need. Is Lauren KIA?" he asked, saying a silent prayer.

"She might make it. Took a really deep stab wound in the gut from a Wolverine ripper claw. Doc is working on her, but she's going to need blood."

"Roger, be there in a minute, the Greens are out of action."

Cordell turned to Sanchez, who had heard the whole conversation. She preempted him by saying, "I've got a whole town to pacify, Carl. You've got the experience. Just try to take one of the Dragons alive, the people need to see that they can be beaten, and they might make good hostages."

"Got it. Wood, Tanchack, let's go. Leave the gun, the militia will take it. Bring the demo."

The three of them hustled down the street, turned the corner, and made their way to the gate. There were Wolverine bodies scattered all over the killing field, and Sergeant Dodson sat against the wall, bandaging his own leg. Beside him, covered in a poncho, was the body of Raj Havner. No one had been able to find any remains of the three NCO's from Team Alpha. Inside the gate, Doc Cofer was bent over Major Cliff, working feverishly under the light of a head lamp, sewing something up in her gut. He sat back with a weary sigh, then started rummaging around in his medkit.

"I'm gonna need some A POS as soon as we can. I sutured up an artery, but she's lost a lot of blood. We'll worry about infection later, I've got nanos running, but they can only do so much with trauma." The medic's hands were dark with blood, and Cordell could see the strain on his face.

"What happened?" he asked, to let him talk.

"She tried to go hand to hand with a Hashut," he answered. "Probably thought she was Zivcovic or something. Dumbass."

"No, she would only do what she had to do." The older man leaned down and squeezed the unconscious woman's hand, whispering, "Hang in there, Lauren."

At the armored door to the building, Blake, Carballo, Sotelo, Wood and Tanchack were discussing how they would clear the building. They had floor plans loaded into their hybrid NVG / Heads Up Displays, and the discussion dwelt on the unknown areas of the lower levels where the Dragons might be.

"What do you think, Erik?" said Cordell as he came up.

"Well, we know there's four Dragons, but their fighting capabilities are unknown. We have a body count that shows at least six Wolverines still alive, their top guys."

Wood spoke up, saying, "I could talk to them, see if they want to surrender."

At that, Carballo snorted. "Get Wolverines to surrender? Shit, brother, even if they wanted to, that pack loyalty shit they've got ain't going to let them, unless the Alpha Dog says so. And that's the Dragons."

"Yeah, well, we can give it a shot. You speak it, so it's on you, Wood. Just don't give 'em any of your government conspiracy bullshit," said the Senior NCO.

"Master Sergeant, I'll do my job, but you know as well as I do that there is some seriously hokey shit that the UN did to undermine United States sovereignty with this made up Inva..." but he stopped when Tanchack put her hand over his mouth.

"Never mind," said Cordell. "Erik, just go in and kill them all. The LT wants some Dragons as prisoners, but I'm not going to cry if they don't make it. I'd say nuke it from orbit, but we want all their tech we can get our hands on, and weapons too."

"Got it. You're staying out for Command & Control. Tanchack, you're the rear and runner if coms won't penetrate the walls." She didn't complain about being selected. Wolverines were no joke, and she knew she didn't have the upper body strength to tangle with one. Everyone had their own skills that made them a team.

"Wood, you're lead, I'm rear, Carballo left and Sotelo right. Wait for my commands for advancing, but shoot everything that moves. Invy or human. Got it?"

"Even slaves?" asked Carballo.

"Do you want to take a chance they haven't got Stockholm syndrome? Or are Green sympathizers?" There was no answer to that.

"OK then, set charges, and on my count of ten, blow it. Let's move!"

Chapter 67

If they had more time, Blake would have preferred they go up onto the roof of the one story building, blow a hole, and drop in. There wasn't enough, though. There never was.

Tanchack was their demo expert, the skill that she brought to the team. She knew, from Cordell's inside information, that the door itself was a no-go. Too thick, armored, and overlapping. No, it would have to be in through the wall, without too much backscatter. She paced off to the left, coming to a spot that she knew opened into a stairwell that headed downward. The team followed and started digging explosive out of their packs.

The red sticks of military grade dynamite had sat, vacuum sealed and locked in an airtight container, for twelve years, since before the invasion. Better than C4 for blowing a hole in concrete, and she chanted the formula under her breath as she lined the sticks up along the wall. "75% RDX, 15% TNT, 5% SAE 10 motor oil, and 5% cornstarch, 75% RDX, 15% TNT, 5% SAE 10 motor oil, and 5% cornstarch," she muttered under her breath.

"Engineers are weird," said Wood as the rest of the team pulled security.

"Pot, Kettle, Black," answered Blake.

Tanchack hesitated, then added five more sticks, crimped in a blasting cap, and ran out a wire spool back to where a claymore detonator lay, outside the gate and around the wall. "OK, now we gotta tamp it. I need as many Wolverine bodies as I can get."

They were used to her asking for weird things, and didn't complain, though the bodies were starting to smell. When she had eight piled up on top of the explosives, the demo sergeant gave the OK. The team started to stack up in a line back from the breech site, preparing to enter the hole, but Tanchack waved them off. "I'm not sure how stable this stuff is; should be OK, but you should be away."

"How far away, Jess?" asked Cordell.

"Like, I dunno, away away. Behind the outer wall, at least."

Blake hesitated. "That kind defeats the purpose of the shock from the explosion."

"Oh," she laughed, "there'll be plenty of shock, trust me. Just be glad there's no rebar, or else this would be complicated."

They moved back behind the wall, and Blake counted down with his fingers, holding them up for everyone to see. At "two", Tanchack hit the clacker, and the ground shook in a deafening blast.

"I MIGHT HAVE USED TOO MUCH!" shouted Tanchack, but no one could hear her over the ringing in their ears.

The assault team ran around the corner of the wall, but stopped when pieces of concrete and Wolverine started raining down on them. Blake shoved them forward, and they ran towards where the corner of the building had been. Instead, there was a grey cloud of dust, making them all choke.

Switching to infrared on their NVG's, the soldiers charged forward, stumbling into the crater where the base of the wall had been, and into the darkness, to be met with a hail of plasma fire. The Wolverines had reacted far faster than they had anticipated, coming down the corridor towards the breech, and the first one to get hit was Sotelo. He and his killer both fired at the same time, the bullets and plasma passing each other in the air, punching through each's body armor, and they died together.

Blake cursed and fired at the figures clustered around the doorway, knocking two down. A return bolt hit Carballo in the foot, taking it off at the ankle. He fell to the floor, rolled, and fired at his attacker, killing the Wolverine. One remained, and this one actually threw its weapon and put its paws up in the air, barking madly. Wood barked back, and the creature laid down on the floor. Carballo sat back up, staring in amazement at the cauterized limb, and then looking over at Sotelo's body. Seeing that the fight was done, he crawled over to his friend. Silent tears streamed down his face as he cradled the dead soldiers' head in his lap.

"Wood, secure that animal!" shouted Blake, and he keyed the team radio. "Doc, Carballo needs attention. Command," he said, forgetting that Major Cliff was wounded, "Sotelo is dead, and I think all the Wolverines are down. We need more support."

"Proceed downstairs, I'll join you, and the militia squad can clear the top floor. Out."

"Just make sure they don't cap our asses when we come back up," answered Blake. Wood had produced a roll of duct tape, and he quickly wrapped the prone Wolverine in it as Tanchack held a rifle on it, but the creature was completely subdued, groveling even.

"Done!" said Wood, and he and the engineer met back up with Blake as Cordell came in through the hole with a half dozen militia and Doc Cofer, who immediately started working on Carballo. The Master Sergeant directed the militia to clear the rest of the upper story, and took his place with Blake, Wood and Tanchack. No words needed to be said; they had been practicing this in out of the way places for almost a decade.

The steps were broad, made for Dragons, not Wolverines. They were approaching the inner sanctum, and each team member felt the tension rise as they proceeded downward. The light changed from Earth normal to a weird bluish white, hotter somehow. At the bottom of the stairs was a steel blast door, with an electronic lock pad set into it. Cordell looked at Tanchack, who merely shook her head. No way to take this one down without blowing the building down around them.

Wood held up his hand and made a "wait a minute gesture", then ran back upstairs. He returned a minute later with the bloody, severed head of a Wolverine.

"It's their Captain, I recognized the rank when I was tying that prisoner up. Let's see what happens." He pried open the bloody eyelid, and held the eye up to the scanner. The rest of the team stepped back, weapons raised.

Chapter 68

The door slid back, and revealed a large room, filled with the weird, oddly rounded computer terminals and display screens the Invy used. On the floor lay the bodies of four Dragons, twisted in the throes of death. Their lasers danced across them, wavering around the room looking for any other threats.

On the floor, scattered about, were the picked clean bones of several humans; sitting on a table was a platter with the upper torso of a teenaged girl. Her eyes were open, and complicated medical equipment ran down into her veins. Blake recognized her as someone who had drifted into town a few weeks ago from a failed farm, and then disappeared. They stared in horror as her eyes blinked, and she mouthed the words, "Help me." She was, Blake realized, about the same age as his son. He raised his rifle, and then lowered it, starting to key his radio for Doc. Instead, Cordell shot the blonde girl through the heart; her body flailed wildly for a second and then her eyes closed, head rolling to one side.

The only other living creature was one of the Octos, arms flailing away at keys and holographic displays. Blake moved to shoot it, but Cordell pushed his rifle down. "We need to take it, if we can," he said.

Tanchack spoke up, saying, "How do we know he'd not calling down a world of shit on us?"

"We don't," answered the Senior NCO. "But big picture. We've never captured one of them alive."

There were two large screens, one showing an orbital track of the Earth. There were only two, not four, and one was highlighted in red. The other screen showed the local area, within a hundred miles. Red icons were blinking at their town, and at several others, that they all knew represented towns with Operational Detachments. The closest, ODA 178, was fifty miles away, to the south. A blue Icon was flashing, only twenty five miles from their position, at the old Joint Base Lewis – McChord.

"That's the Invy Quick Reaction Force for the area, four APC's, two tanks, and a full company of Wolverines" said Blake. "They'll come here first." As if it could hear them, the Octo swiped at the screens, making them disappear. Then, strangely, it looked at them for a long moment. Tanchack moved to grab at it, and the creature stiffened and fell dead.

The lights went out and all the computer screens went blank. "That's not good!" said Wood. They didn't need to say why it wasn't. All four just flipped down their NVG's, turned, and fled up the stairs. Gunfire sounded louder as they jogged upwards, the shallow, wide steps throwing off their stride.

"MILITIA LEADER!" called Cordell over the squad radio, "PULL BACK, NOW! COFER, GET THE CASUALTIES BACK TO THE TOWN." They stopped at the top of the stairs, waiting by the demolished wall. The town militia appeared in twos and threes, one pair carrying a body, and the Operators hustled them out, waiting until the squad leader appeared, and they broke into a run.

They made it all the way back to where the destroyed MK-19 was, their designated rally point just around the corner, waiting for a blast. And waited. Even as they did, they could hear random shots as Lt. Sanchez and her squad, accompanied by the militia troops, secured the town.

"It's not going to blow," said Tanchack. "I didn't see any explosives wired to critical structures…" she started to say, when the ground shook, and the building seemed to lift up, then settle back down inward on itself. A soft "WHOOMP" reached them at the same time.

Wood laughed and said, "Well, you know the Illuminati aren't going to want us find out this was all bullshit anyway."

Blake just shook his head, and turned to Cordell. "What's next, boss?"

"We have to go reinforce the guys that are going to take on the armor; if we can't get some air support from Cascades base, those tanks are going to chew them up."

They gathered together the militia, about a dozen men and women, and ran back to the concealed warehouse. Once there, Blake took charge off distributing the heavier weapons. He was startled to realize that the whole action so far had only taken about twenty minutes, and he wondered how his son was doing. Never mind that, he thought as he slung a Javelin launcher on his back, and refilled his water. Killing was thirsty work.

The ambush site had been pre-selected, as with everything else. Almost ten years in place gives you a lot of time to do some sneaking and peeking, and planning. Six months ago, when word had come that Red Dawn was finally happening, Tanchack and Wood had carefully cached explosives at the base of a bridge where I-5 crossed over the Nisqually River. Lt. Sanchez had dispatched Sergeant Patton and more militia to fill Captain Ellison and his veterans in on the plan, and they had to hustle to get there; it was over two kilometers away. No joke carrying a launcher and ammunition, in the dark

Wood struggled with the heavy directional EMP, but it was vital that the weapon be brought along. The Invy drones needed to be taken out as soon as the ambush was initiated, or before if possible. Standard Invy practice was to have anything bigger than a patrol accompanied by UAV's, including one about a klick in advance to scout ahead.

When they finally got there, the light of false dawn was showing in the East, and Mt. Rainier loomed bulky in the darkness, blocking out the stars. Blake slipped into the prepared fighting position, ordering the militia members in it to move out to the right and left and provide fire support. Tanchack slid in next to him, and dug around for the buried wires that lead to the charges, several hundred meters away. She hoped desperately that some animal hadn't broken them in the week since she had last checked.

Both were soaked with sweat, and rapidly chilled in the cool October air. It was the nature of what they did, hurry up and wait, but they didn't have long. The IR sensor on their NVG's picked up the hot plume of air cushioned vehicles approaching down the battered highway.

"Well," said Tanchack, brushing a stray blonde hair out of her eyes. "At least we're done waiting."

"You know," said Blake, keeping his eye to the sight, "you're OK."

"Gee, thanks. I think."

Their conversation ceased as the first APC hovered into view. Overhead, an orbital crested the horizon to the west, and long streaks of fire started to fall from the sky, headed towards the northeast.

"HQ is going to get it," said the engineer, hand on the detonator.

Blake said nothing. It was time. They both watched as the armor approached the bridge. Their dug in overhead cover kept the drones from seeing them, but as soon as the attackers fired, their muzzle flashes would give them away.

Wood fired first; the EMP was based on the old Stinger anti-aircraft system, adapted by Raytheon to carry a limited range Electro Magnetic Pulse warhead. Instead of acquiring a heat source, though, the seeker looked for electrical signals being generated by the drones, and rocketed off in the general direction of the convoy. It detonated with the slightest of sparks, but sent out an Electro Magnetic Pulse that disabled unshielded circuits within a few hundred meters, depending on conditions. The armored vehicles were shielded from the effects, but the two drones accompanying them fell from the sky.

"Game on, Bro!" shouted Tanchack, and she hit the clacker.

The bridge didn't explode sky high like some Hollywood movie. Instead, there were a series of flashes and muted CRUMPS, and it tilted to one side. The lead tank slid slowly to the left, engine whining in protest, then fell thirty feet to the ground, landing on its side in the river and disappearing into the mud. The APC behind it managed to swerve right, the driver hoping to get to firmer pavement, but with a thunderous crash, the entire bridge let go. The second APC followed the first down into the river.

With a WHOOSH, POP! Blake let fly with the first Javelin. Not looking to see if it hit, he slapped Tanchack on the shoulder, dropped the weapon, detached the sight, and the two of them scrambled from the hole, diving into another prepared position ten meters to the left. The spot they had just left erupted into a shower of dirt and melted rock from a large bore plasma bolt, the tank in the third position having seen the launch. Behind it, one APC was firing an automatic grenade launcher at the militia positions slightly below the hole the two Operators sheltered in. The fifth vehicle, the last ACP, burned brightly, blocking any escape the other two might have had back down the highway.

Blake worked feverishly to fix the sight to the launcher tube, cursing as the thirty year old equipment failed to gain a connection signal. He picked up a rock and hammered on the sight, and the screen lit up. His next target, the remaining tank, fired again, the big round hammering into a bunker that had held a machine gun and three militia.

The grenades were keeping the return fire down, and Blake could see the forms of multiple Wolverines snaking their way through the grass on the far side of the river. Some had already swum across, and were headed across the valley towards them. Ignoring the infantry, he sighted on the tank, got a lock, and fired. Out of missiles, he dropped the entire unit and ran backwards, not waiting to see what the effect of his attack was.

He stopped when he realized that Tanchack wasn't with him, spun, and ran back. She was still in the hole, firing her rifle at the Wolverines. Then he saw his missile impact on the top of the tank, just as it let loose another round from its cannon. His friend disappeared in a gout of flame and dirt, and Blake was hurled backwards, ears ringing, his whole body numb from the concussion, and he blacked out.

When he woke, men were running past him, to the rear. They had broken; the Wolverines were flailing the ridge with accurate plasma fire, and the remaining APC had crossed the river, firing at anything human sized its sensors saw moving. Blake started to climb to his feet, but felt nauseous. He leaned over and threw up, just as Sergeant Wood kneeled down next to him. The NCO fired his rifle, and grabbed Blake by the harness, dragging him, half stumbling, backwards. Thoughts of his son raced through Eric Blake's' mind, and he guessed he would never see him again.

His NVG's had been torn away by the blast, but dawn was growing in the east, allowing him to see where he and Wood were going. They followed the retreating militia, dropping down the crest of a small hill that the highway cut through. Blake was exhausted, and he held up his hand to the other man. "Gimme you rifle, Wood, and get the fuck out of here. That's an order."

The younger man smiled, and answered, "No last stands for you, old man. Just a few more meters," and continued to half push, half carry Blake down the slope. They made it behind the wreck of an old, rusty car, one of dozens that lined the sides of the highway, shoved there by the military before the Invy landed, after the strikes. As Blake tried to focus, head still buzzing from the blast, he saw the top of the APC come over the crest of the hill, with a dozen Wolverines flanking on either side. He dragged out his pistol and started firing in the direction of the attacking Invy, but couldn't focus on a target. Next to him, Wood's rifle barked out a steady staccato of single shots. Return fire forced their heads down, plasma bolts hitting the metal and throwing of sparks.

Wood turned, cupped his hands around his mouth, and yelled "NOW!" at the top of his lungs. A beam of pure fire lanced out from behind one of the wrecks, as Master Sergeant Cordell let loose with a salvaged Invy anti-tank launcher. The short range weapon hit the front armor of the APC, drilled through, and then impacted the antimatter containment unit that powered the fans. With a thunderous roar, the APC cracked open in a brilliant flash of light.

The militia, who Blake had seen running away a minute before, poured fire into the flanks of the Wolverines advancing forward, killing a half dozen in an instant. Then a string of claymore mines, set into the sides of the road and wired onto wrecks, banged in unison, cutting down more of the aliens. The rest, for the first time since the Invasion, broke and ran.

Blake reloaded his pistol, stood, and tried to fire at the backs of the enemy. The world swam in front of him and, blood flowing freely from an unfelt splinter of rock that had penetrated his leg, Sergeant First Class Eric Blake fell over sideways. He stared at the lightening sky and the fading stars, said his sons' name once, and the world went black.

Chapter 70

Light shone in through a window as the sun dropped down behind the Olympic Mountains, sinking towards the hidden Pacific Ocean. Erik Blake woke slowly, tried to sit up, reaching for a weapon, then realized where he was. He laid back down on the bed and stared at the ceiling. Well, he was alive, even though he felt like crap. He had been wounded before, in the Spratleys, shot in the abdomen, and waking up from that had felt like hell. Today, he was weak, and his leg hurt, but, well, good enough.

The town clinic was a bare bones affair, since they had little to no medical supplies. Their team medic, Doc Cofer, had acted as the town's only doctor, doing everything from surgery to amputations to delivering babies. He sat in a chair on the other side of the room, covered in blood and snoring loudly.

In the bed next to him was Sergeant Carballo, eating a sandwich. The stump of his foot was elevated up on a pillow. He leaned over and offered it to Blake, who shook his head.

"Suit yourself," said Carballo, and shoved more in his mouth.

"Doesn't that hurt?" asked Blake, gesturing to the missing foot.

"Dude," said the soldier, between chewing, "I am high as a goddamned kite right now."

In the farther bed, past Carballo, Lauren Cliff lay still as death under clean sheets. Her chest gently rose and fell; an IV hung from a pole, replacing lost blood. One side of her face was swollen beyond recognition, and there was an ugly cut running down her face.

From his right, there was a cough, and Blake turned to see Master Sergeant Cordell gazing out the window. His team sergeant turned back to him, a sad look on his dark face. The man looked like he had aged a dozen years in the last twenty four hours. Gunfire sounded outside, muted single shots, in a measured pace.

"What's going on?" asked Blake. "Is there still fighting?"

"Regime change. History repeating itself," Cordell sighed. "The LT gave up trying to stop them about an hour ago. The Greens have been abusing these people for a long time."

"Jesus," said Blake, then nothing else.

Cordell pulled up a chair, turned it around, and sat. Then he said bluntly, "Alex and several of his friends took off early this morning, while we were at the ambush site. We think they're heading towards Portland, but I don't think they'll get far."

The news hit Blake like a hammer, but he should have seen it coming. He and his son had increasingly been arguing about it, about what the Invy claimed they were there for. When Scout Team Eleven had come through two years ago, and shared the photographic evidence of the Invy slave sites and the fighting pits, he had been very tempted to share them with him. When had seen the body of the young girl last night, and the bones scattered about, the veteran NCO had felt sick. Not from the carnage, but from the thought of his own kid lying there.

Blake started to get up, muttering, "I gotta go find him!" and the room swam around him. Cordell helped him lie back down, then stood up.

"I'll find him, Erik," he said. "The LT has already given me permission; I'm going to take Wood out with me after we get some rest."

Blake pushed his feelings way down deep, as he had done earlier that night. "Can you give me a SITREP?"

"Well, we haven't heard from Cascadia HQ since early this morning, pretty sure they took some hits. We had brief ham radio contact with Raven Rock, they just gave the code to Charlie Mike, then went off the air"

"The orbitals?"

Cordell shook his head. "There's still one overhead. Hasn't dropped any rods, but they could be out of ammo. Dunno."

"And local?" asked Blake, grateful for whatever took his mind off his son.

"We got a runner come up from Portland, hauled ass on a motorcycle. The attack there failed, and they need some help. The Invy hold the town, and they're massacring the civilians. Apparently someone warned them just before the attack."

"Well," said Blake, "we can't win everywhere."

Cordell shook his head. The man looked extremely tired, and he took a long moment to answer. "Erik, this is going to be a very long war. Get some rest; I'm going to need you. Doc says you should be out of bed in a day or two. The militia are going to pull out in a day or so to give some help securing JBLM, see what's left there. Good job on the ambush, that armor could have screwed us royally."

Blake closed his eyes, but it didn't make the scene of Tanchack getting vaporized disappear from his mind. "Who else?"

"Major Cliff is going to be touch and go. Infection is going to be the big thing; if we get control of the airspace, and HQ is still around, I'll see if I can get her a medevac to the base hospital. Patton caught a burst in the ambush, he's gone. Dodson is mobile, but Doc was pulling parts of the 19 out of his leg. Lynch, Prael and Tyler are splattered all over the wall of the building where the APC detonated."

My God, thought Blake. More than half the team dead or wounded. "It's going to be tough to control the town with only a few effectives," he said, thinking out loud.

"We're done here, Erik" said Cordell. "The Invy aren't going to come back for this town, and we have other targets. This was only the first shots of the campaign, and I doubt any of us are going to live to see the end of it."

He stood up and put his hand on his subordinate's shoulder. "I'll find your son, and then, fragos not withstanding, we're going to join up with the Main Force unit out of Tacoma and hit every Invy base we can in the Puget Sound area. We've got an army to build, so rest up."

Chapter 71

Johanna Sanchez watched the sun disappear over the mountains. It had been a very long, very exhausting day. Cursing the lack of coffee for the thousandth time in the last hour, she rubbed dirty hands across her face. She was really this close to shooting the loudmouth bastard in front of her running his trap.

"Listen, Bob, I don't care about who runs this town. You're liberated, hold a goddamned election or something. We have a war to fight."

"How the hell do we know you're even with the CEF? You're just a whore!" he spluttered. Unlike a lot of the towns' people, he wasn't rail thin from scraping through harvests. Bob Paulis was a trader, digging through ruins to find small things that weren't banned by the Invy, but made life a little easier. He had lived a life of comparative ease, compared to many, but had never actually collaborated.

"No, I'm a soldier who did what she had to do to accomplish her mission. Like all of you think you had to do," she answered, nodding towards the blindfolded bodies lying boneless in the dirt. Most were men, and a few wore Green armbands. Several, though, were women, teachers in the Invy school. She had tried to stop them, but their blood was up, and she wasn't going to shoot townspeople who were correcting past injustices. The right way would have been a trial, but there was no time for that, and no place to hold so many prisoners anyway.

No, she just had to wash her whole hands of the thing. She wasn't going to let this blowhard call her a whore, though. She lifted her pistol and pointed it directly at the man's face, cocked back the hammer, and said, "Shut the fuck up before I put another useless hole in your ugly mug, asshole!"

He did, and pissed himself in the process. She lowered the pistol and uncocked it, slipping it back into her leg holster. "Listen up!" she called to the several hundred men and women milling around in the town square. "My team is going to head out of here soon enough. Captain Ellis will be back in about a half an hour with the rest of the militia. Martial law is in effect, and you can take all this up with him."

"Can you tell us what's happening in the outside world?" asked an older woman.

Sanchez shook her head. "No Ma'am. Our comms with headquarters was cut off early this morning. But as you can see, there's only one orbital left in the sky, and they haven't fired anything in hours. I think we may have a chance of winning."

"But, even if we do, what then?" asked the woman, a puzzled look on her face.

Sanchez shrugged and answered, "That's not my problem." Then she motioned to Wood, who had a disgusted look on his face. He gave the finger to Paulis, and, with Chu, they left to go to clinic. Dodson met them at the door, hobbling on crutches.

They came in just as Cordell finished explaining the situation to Blake. They woke up Doc, and the team had a quick huddle. What was left of the team, anyway.

"OK, listen up," said Sanchez. "We've got twenty four hours to rest and refit, and then we head out to Tacoma."

"What about down by Portland?" asked Blake.

"They're going to have to deal with things on their own. We have to link up with the Main Force in Tacoma; no idea how their attack on SeaTac went. Colonel Maitland," meaning the Main Force CO, "is going to need every trained swinging dick he can get, and we've got to get that prisoner to Cascadia."

"Well, I guess that leaves yourself and Chu out," said Cordell, with a tired grin.

That brought a chuckle out of the team, and Wood said, "Old man's got jokes!"

"Erik, while we're gone, you're in charge, until Lauren is back on her feet. Stay out of the town politics as best you can. Work with Captain Ellis to start forming a real light infantry company."

"About my son…" said Blake.

"A dozen kids went with him. They headed south on I-5; the guy from Portland saw them on his way through. Me and Wood will find them."

"Wood and I," said the younger NCO.

"If I wanted shit from you, Eddie, I'd squeeze your head," answered Cordell.

***

"There they are," said Wood, designating the group huddled at the base of a tree with his IR laser. The teens were oblivious to their approach, talking quietly amongst themselves. It was five miles south of the town.

"Alex! This is Master Sergeant Cordell, your dad sent me." At his voice, the teens all stood up and looked around wildly, until Wood turned on his Taclight and shone it in their faces.

"Are … are you going to kill us?" asked a girl.

"Eddie, turn the light off." Cordell cracked a glow stick and set it down on the ground. "No we're not going to kill you. Alice, isn't it? Gina Pavone's daughter?"

"Yy,yes," she answered.

"We're here to bring you home," he said.

"BULLSHIT!" said an angry looking kid, his features twisted in the green light. "You're a bunch of murderers!"

"Probably right," answered Wood. "War's an ugly business, son."

"I'm not your son!" he replied angrily.

"No, but if you were, I'd beat your ass."

"Sergeant Wood," said Cordell, "how about we take these kids to that site we found behind the power plant?"

"Good idea, Master Sergeant. I don't know who created the Invy, but any which way, they're scum."

By the time they got to where they wanted to go, the kids were stumbling, and two were crying. Wood flicked his light on, and swept it around.

What he revealed was carnage. Piles of picked clean bones lay all about, and two corpses were strung up from a metal girder, arms hanging down. One was still dressed in the green coveralls that all the teens wore to school, but both were headless.

"Oh, oh my God!" shrieked the girl named Alice. Then she threw up, and the angry boy fainted.

"Where's my dad?" asked Alex, when Wood turned off the light.

Cordell was silent, then said, "He's at the clinic. He was wounded in…" but he didn't get to finish his answer. Alex Blake took off running.

"DAD!" he yelled, throwing up the door before Dodson could get up from the chair in the hallway. He ran into the ward, and stopped when he saw Major Cliff, lying there hideously wounded. Looking wildly around, he saw his father at the far end. He rushed over and buried his face on his Erik's chest.

"It's OK, buddy, it's OK," whispered Erik Blake, holding his son tightly. And it was.

Part V

"Thunder Run"

Just south of the Invy base at SeaTac Airport, Seattle, Washington

My heart is broken by the terrible loss I have sustained in my old friends and companions and my poor soldiers. Believe me, nothing except a battle lost can be half so melancholy as a battle won: the bravery of my troops hitherto saved me from the greater evil; but to win such a battle as this of Waterloo, at the expense of so many gallant friends, could only be termed a heavy misfortune but for the result to the public.

~Arthur Wellesley, 1st Duke of Wellington, 1815

Chapter 72

The tank sat there waiting, massive, and seemingly immobile. Marks on the concrete showed where the treads had moved seventy tons of weight, some dozen years ago. Since then, it had moved, but only a little. Enough to exercise the hydraulics, keep the treads from rusting in place.

She had rolled off the factory floor more than half a century ago, armed with a 105mm rifled cannon. Her first years were spent staring at the Fulda Gap, waiting for the Soviet tank armies to roll through, and waiting patiently. Those also serve who only stand and wait.

First blood came at the battle of 73 Easting, her upgraded 120mm smoothbore gun hurling a depleted uranium dart at over five thousand feet per second. In a bloody hour, the cream of the Iraqi Republican Guard was shattered in a rain of hell. Her enemies never knew what hit them, far outranging anything else.

A decade later, she drove over the familiar crust of desert, hammering her way up the Euphrates river valley. She was wounded, a T-72 main gun round shattering a track, but her gunner blew the attacker away, and she and her sisters rolled triumphant through streets that had first been conquered almost a thousand years ago by Mongol hordes.

Then the endless war. Sitting at check points, scanning, waiting, her might too much for the insurgents. Not the kind of combat she longed for. Instead, her lesser guns chattered into the night, easily fending off attackers whose ancestors who had withstood the phalanxes of Alexander the Great, two millennia before.

She returned to her home, to the factory where she was born, and received more upgrades, better protection, and was transferred to the US Marine Corps, to storm ashore in the Philippines, slugging it out toe to toe with equals, receiving many wounds in the process, but coming back alive, covered with glory. The dried blood of her crew still lingered on in small crevices, each forever a part of her now.

Then, power was ripped from her. The turbine that had served her so well for decades was replaced by a barely controlled heart of annihilation, and electricity coursed through new drive motors, spinning her tracks at a furious rate. There was talk of replacing the gun, but in the end, the new technology was too fragile, too complicated, but she was satisfied with tried and true. A new skin joined the alternating dozen layers of paints, one that was alive with light and darkness, one that draped and concealed her angular profile.

"Goddamn, but you're beautiful," said the Maintenance Chief, wiping his hands on a rag. "OK, LIGHT HER UP!" he yelled.

The driver, her brown hair confined by a CVC, reached down and flipped switches, and the antimatter reactor crackled to life. The PFC could feel it, the stray wisps of her hair waving around her face with static.

"OK, bring her forward, now back, left track, right track, OK, good to go!" shouted the Chief over the whine. He gave a thumbs up to the Tank Commander, who was sitting half out of her hatch. Sergeant First Class Lisa Dash smiled, broad grin splitting dark features, and yelled down a command to the gunner.

The turret spun a full three hundred and sixty degrees, then the gun rose and fell. From her position, Dash flipped a switch, and the tank seemed, to the Chief, to almost melt into the background of the rough cavern walls. The track commander climbed down and ran her hand along the gun barrel, reading the words stenciled there, *BAD BITCH*. There were twenty two kill rings behind the nickname. "It's been a long time, but we gots work to do, honey. Gonna smack some dat Invy ass." She almost felt the M1A6 Abrams tank rumble in reply.

The Chief walked over as the loader climbed out of his own hatch, followed by the gunner. "Ibson, he said to the loader, "doesn't it bother you to be the only guy in an all-girl crew?"

"No, except when they all cycle at the same time," laughed the Canadian. "It's like living with my sisters, you know when to clear out of the house."

His gunner punched him, hard. "He fits in just fine, with his girlie name, Chief. Who names their boy Jamie, anyway? Silly foreigner, get out, eh?"

Corporal Ibson picked up the gunner and slung her over his shoulder, then spun in circles, and put her down gently. "Now let me see you hit something, Dizzy!" he laughed.

The maintenance warrant officer smiled; it was good to see a tight crew. The driver, PFC Banks, knew her stuff, despite living in the ruins of Tacoma. When the recall of the Main Force unit had come last week, she had taken to the simulator like she was born to it. The gunner, Sergeant Lehmkuhl, was the epitome of the dizzy blonde, but as a nineteen year old Lance Corporal in the Spratly War, she had killed five Chinese tanks in the battle of Manilla. This while the headless torso of her track commander sat between her and the loader, hand cranking the turret around. In other times, she would have received the Medal of Honor, but all that was forgotten in the invasion.

"Dash," said chief, "sign off on this, and I can release her to you. I've got three others to deal with, and only twelve hours to do it."

"All your damn paperwork. The world done ended, mon, an we still gotta do paperwork!" she said with her lilting Jamaican accent.

"We're going to strangle the Invy with it," laughed the chief, but he still stood there with the tablet held out. She grimaced, and ran the stylus over the screen. Freaking cavemen probably had to chisel their mark on stone to get their spears, she thought.

The warrant smiled, turned the tablet off, said, "She's all yours!" and walked over to the next Abrams. Dash watched him go and then turned to her crew.

"OK, let's load her up! I wants half sabot and the rest HEAT and canister, and enough small ammo so her bellies done scrape de ground!" In her excitement, her accent had gotten worse, even though she was a long way from the Caribbean. It was time for revenge. It was time to kill.

Dash laid her hand on the cool metal, ran it lightly across the mottled green and brown active camouflage, causing it to ripple under her hand, individual nodes of LED's flaring to life briefly. Not perfect, but it would have to do. Every advantage they could get over the Invy would help, but she put her faith in balls to the wall, straight up charging in. She had seen it at the battle of Cheyenne Mountain; they had fought the bastards to a standstill, and then ripped the heart out of the attackers, before hell had dropped from the sky.

"Yes," she whispered, "you and me, Bad Bitch, we 'bout to kick some alien ass, ole girl." Small charges of static seemed to answer, eagerly.

Chapter 73

Before they rolled out, Dash called the crew together at the front of the tank. They had all been training together for years, in preparation for today's work. Except for Banks, they were all veterans of the Invasion War; Lehmkuhl and Dash had both fought in the Spratly War, though Dash had been an artillery section chief. Her Spratly war had been spent mostly in a Chinese POW camp, after that first disastrous battle in Taiwan. Still, she knew how important motivation was to accomplishing a mission. She didn't doubt their individual spark, but they needed to be a team, completely.

"Listen, kids, to your momma Lisa. Dis is gonna be a real tough fight, and we gonna bunks dem Invy real bad, so listen you up," she began, but Banks raised her hand.

"Sarge," she said, "can you drop the Jamaican accent? I, like, have no idea what you, like, just said."

Dash laughed, and said, "Sure, Terry. I can speak American better than you can, if that helps."

Banks scowled and said, "Ain't my fault, ain't like there's any schoolin in the ruins."

Theresa Banks was nineteen years old; the rest of the crew were in their thirties or, like Dash, an ancient forty. She had little memory of the war, or even of life before it. When the Main Force recruiters had found her, Banks was scavenging already picked over Walmarts in Tacoma, leading a small gang of kids in vicious territorial battles with other almost savages. Seeing her natural leadership ability, the recruiters had grabbed her at night and hauled her, sedated, to their base.

It took a while for her anger to abate, but over the last year, a world had been opened up to her, one she barely knew had existed. She had taken to the tank simulator immediately, and had been up for early promotion to gunner when the order for Red Dawn came.

"You're doing fine, Terry. Once we beat these bastards, I'll help you get a degree and get into officer's school. It's going to be a long war for all of us, and long after I'm too old to be climbing up and down this tank, you'll be kicking ass and taking back everything they done took from all of us."

Banks smiled back at her, and Dash was struck by how young she looked. Just a kid, should be going to college and dreaming dreams of a family, she thought. Not riding out to meet the devil.

"So listen to me now," the SFC continued. "We going to be heading into hell, the likes of which some of us haven't faced before. It's OK to be scared, because we know a soldiers' got a right to be scared, but I'm not saying anyone can back out. We's a team, and we's going to fight like a team."

Erica "Dizzy" Lehmkuhl wasn't scared. She should have been dead long ago, in her mind. In the P.I. and later at the battle of Cheyenne Mountain. She and Dash had fought the Invy together then, as gunner and tank commander, escaped the chaos of defeat to return here, and she trusted her now. Battle would come, and that icy, cool feeling would descend over her like a blanket. She looked Dash right in the eye, and neither woman said anything, until her chief winked, and Dizzy smiled back, a grim smile. They both knew the price they might pay.

"Can we, you know, just get this over with?" interjected Ibson. "I want to get back to issuing warnings to rude people, once my great country has been restored to peace and tranquility."

"I bet you have your Mountie uniform just hanging in the closet, all shiny and shit!" said Lehmkuhl.

"And, why not? If we win, Vancouver is going to need some good law and order again. Just you wait." From there, the two devolved into good natured insults, with Banks egging them on.

Dash left the crew to picking on each other, and went to meet with the other tank commanders for a final briefing. It was short, there were only five tanks. The mechanized infantry were having their own last minute conference.

Her Captain was a good officer, but a crappy tanker, with no experience. He had wanted Dash to be his gunner, but somehow, it just didn't work out that way. She had her crew, and she didn't give good odds to him making it through the fight. He hadn't seemed to learn the balance between command of a unit and command of a tank. Always, in the simulators, ignoring unit matters to give commands to his driver one minute, then jumping back on the net the next. He needed to either do one, as a sergeant, or the other, as an officer.

"Sergeant Dash, any input?" he asked, but before she could say anything, he turned to ask something of *Orca*'s TC. Then he ignored him and moved to another, like he was just running through a drill. She felt sorry for the crew of *Ragnar,* his tank. They were interrupted when the Regimental Commander pulled her boss aside for his own pep talk.

Dash reached out and hugged each of her fellow tank commanders in turn. She had known them for years, and odds are, this was the last day any of them would see. Then she knelt, and, regardless of their faith, said a prayer for each. Their respect for her was enough that they all bowed their heads. In her deep voice, she recited,

I have fought when others feared to serve.
I have gone where others failed to go.
I've lost friends in war and strife,
Who valued Duty more than love of life.

I have shared the comradeship of pain.
I have searched the lands for men that we have lost.
I have friends who served this land of liberty,
Who would fight to see that other stricken lands are free.

I have seen the weak forsake humanity.
I have heard the traitors praise our enemy.
I've seen challenged men become even bolder,
I've seen the Duty, Honor, Sacrifice of the Soldier.

Now I understand the meaning of our lives,
The loss of comrades not so very long ago.
So to you who have answered duty's siren call,
May God bless us all, may God bless us all.

"And,' she continued, "if I don't make it back, I'll see you on Fiddler's Green soon enough."

"You better have a cold beer waiting, Lisa!" answered *Selchie*'s commander.

"Gonna have some Red Stripe, um hum!" she smiled back at the woman.

Suzie Q's boss said, "Ugh, not that piss!" and they all laughed.

From speakers overhead, the Regimental Commanders' voice boomed, *"RIFLES! MOUNT UP!"*

They all bumped fists, shouted "BAD BITCH!" and rode to death and ruin.

Chapter 74

In the distance, she could see the outline of the broken Space Needle, lit by the setting moon. Though Seattle had taken a number of orbital strikes, the Invy had concentrated on hitting the numerous military bases instead of civilian populace. Joint Base Lewis-McChord, Whidbey Island Naval Air Station, Kitsap, Everett, they had all taken a pounding, even the Boeing manufacturing facilities. Except for a small area of JBLM that the Invy used to house a mechanized platoon, all their local forces were concentrated at the old SeaTac airport. The runway there was long enough that their cargo lifters, massive multi engine ships assisted by antigravity, could get a boost lifting off, carrying the loot of Earth.

Their attack was scheduled to coincide with the submarines' firing on the orbital stations. Dash knew that if it worked, then they had a chance. If it didn't, well, no matter what their efforts amounted to, it was all over. A devout Catholic, she said a quick Hail Mary as they reached the last hill before their final run into the base and came to a stop in defilade. Behind the four tanks spread out three Bradley Fighting Vehicles and a half dozen wheeled Strykers, carrying the Main Force infantry soldiers of the 1/161st Infantry, the Highlanders. The runway at SeaTac was about ten miles away, through the ruins of the suburbs of Seattle. The men and women in the infantry were going to be advancing over ruins that had been, once, their homes.

The movements had been timed so that they came to rest minutes before each orbital passed overhead, the armor coming to a squeaking halt, cooling sprays venting their excess engine heat. That problem had taken a long time to solve, and the chemicals used in the dispersal were some really bad shit. The VA would probably deny their claims when they all died of cancer in a few years, Dash mused to herself as she idly sat watching the countdown.

Behind them, about three miles to the rear, crewmembers were slowly placing their hands on elevation wheels, getting ready to start engines to provide hydraulic power, and silently screwing Variable Timed fuses on 155 caliber artillery rounds. Artillery had done little good against the first invasion, mobile as it was, but here it was to keep the defenders' heads down while the tanks advanced. The six surviving Paladins of the 2nd Battalion, 146th Field Artillery Regiment had firing solutions for every square meter of the base. The howitzers had been emplaced a week before, step by step, hiding from orbitals, going places the Invy patrols ignored.

Scout Team Eleven, four miles closer to the base, watched through night vision as an Invy foot patrol made its way out of the perimeter. On any other night, the scouts would have quietly slipped away, gathering information on times and routes, but not tonight. Each member of the seven man team held one of the Invy in their sights, and would fire the first suppressed shots of the early morning.

The battle, like any combined arms battle, would be a dance carefully coordinated by the Regimental Commander. Timing was everything, and Dash had the plan memorized in her head, but the veteran knew that it would all go out the window as soon as the dance started.

At H minus thirty seconds, all across the Puget Sound area, radio sets with pre-programmed, semi intelligent software started broadcasting back and forth, simulating a massive wave of communications traffic. An orbital had just crested the horizon; the hope was that the Invy would be unable to identify the real chatter from fake, and be overwhelmed by targets. Some were stationary, while others moved cross country on small wheeled drones.

At H minus fifteen seconds, Dash turned on her radio in time to hear the Regimental Commander call, *"Execute, and Godspeed, Rifle Six, out."* At the same moment, she felt the rumble of the artillery firing through the soles of her boots, slightly shaking the seventy ton tank. The rounds passing overhead made their characteristic ripping sound, and she hit the lever dropping her back into the tank, pulling the hatch shut after her and activating her helmet mounted display. External sensors, modeled off the F-35 program, seemed to make the tank around her invisible, showing her a 360 view of the outside, turning night into day.

"KICK IT, BITCH!" she yelled, half to the driver, and half to the tank, and PFC Banks twisted the grip, engaging the drive. Lehmkuhl already had her helmet mounted display going, and the turret tracked side to side as she looked for targets, following the movement of her head. Ibson sat ready, his job the least high tech of all, ready to open the door with his knee switch, select whatever round his commander asked for, and muscle it into the breech. A HEAT round was already loaded, giving them the best option against any targets they might face.

They were all thrown backwards by the acceleration, and could hear Banks give a whoop! of joy as they tore down the highway. One thing that the designers had never really overcome was the rough ride of any tracked vehicle, and the highway was full debris. There was a discernable lane through the wrecks, though; they Main Force soldiers had spent the last nine years surreptitiously moving them around to provide a semi clear lane.

Behind *Bad Bitch* in the lead came her sisters, *Orca, Suzie Q, Selchie,* and *Balrog.* Each tank had their guns aimed to one side or another, covering their sectors, and Dash took a second to look behind her, her chest swelling with pride. Finally, finally, finally.

The sixth vehicle in their column was their air defense, a bigger version of the EMP generator the ODA teams had. It crested the hill, lit up its radar and immediately started knocking drones out of the sky. After ten seconds, the firing stopped and the Stryker vehicle moved out again.

The Abrams reached a bone jarring speed, crashing over piles of rubble and through ditches, the stabilized main gun tilting up and down in time with Lehmkuhl' aiming point. Dash, though, was to draw first blood. She was scanning her head in a counter point motion to her gunner, and caught a glimpse of a shape starting to lift into the sky. Slapping the joystick into her hand, she overrode Lehmkuhl's sight, yelled, "FROM MY POSITION, AIRCRAFT, ON THE WAY!", flipped a switch that set the fuse to proximity and triggered the gun.

The cannon lurched backwards, causing an enormous flash to light the night, accompanied by an incredibly loud CRACK!, and the HEAT round ripped through the air. Sergeant First Class Lisa Dash thought for a brief moment of her childhood in poverty, leaving Jamaica to come to America, how she had earned her college degree through serving in the Washington Army National Guard, and built her own business and family. It had all been torn from her, her husband, her two daughters, and she threw back her head and laughed as the round intersected the flight path of the Invy ship. A second tank also fired, and the wingman peeled off east, leaving a glowing trail of sparks that, after a few seconds, erupted into a blinding flash of antimatter annihilation.

Lisa Dash laughed on and on, consumed by the joy of revenge as they pulled into their first pre-sighted firing position.

Chapter 75

"RELOAD, SABOT!" Dash yelled, the laughter still continuing in her head. Ibson already had the door open, and his fingers punched the selector, making the bottom of the round pop outwards. He hauled mightily on it with his right hand on the base and his left on the top, then flipped it around, smoothly ramming it into the open mouth of the gun. His final act was to pull his hand away as the heavy steel breech swung closed.

"UP!" he yelled, and Dizzy yelled "ON THE WAY!" The gun rocked backwards, the tank with it, pushing it down onto its springs. Dash could have demanded that the gunner run through the standard fire commands, but she trusted Dizzy Lehmkuhl to do a good job. Hers was to keep them alive. Ibson didn't wait for a command either; from here on out it was Sabot until either the gunner or the commander ordered differently. Fine by him.

"Driver, back up!" she ordered, as return fire started to come their way. Their opposition was a company of Invy tanks, if the crews managed to get to them before the artillery cut them down. She had to assume they would face the full dozen the Invy organized their companies in, though. The Abrams dropped backwards, and she started to give the driver commands to maneuver them to the next spot, when the left side of her vision temporarily whited out, accompanied by an explosion that rocked Bad Bitch sideways on her tracks.

A hundred meters away the turret of *Suzie Q* leapt upward into the air, flipped over twice, and then fell back on top of the hull, almost snuffing out the fire that raged inside. The track commander, less experienced than Dash, had let his driver expose the shot trap, the space between the hull and the turret, while scanning for targets. The 100mm plasma bolt had blown through the drivers' head, under the main gun, across the loader, and hit the anti-matter reactor that drove the tank. The resulting explosion had come back into the crew compartment and vented its fury in that contained space, incinerating the crew and lifting the forty ton turret high into the air.

She had no time to mourn her friends, just fight the tank. They were to engage at long distance, draw the enemies' fire while the infantry swung wide around the base. Could be that, tonight, nobody was going to get out of here alive, but she'd take some of the bastards with her. *Bad Bitch* rolled fifty meters west, shielded by the hill, and then moved though the ruin of a house, the muzzle of her gun being given a narrow view to scan.

Lehmkuhl caught a glimpse of the angular side of an Invy tank also shifting position, rotating on its air cushion, and fired, the sabot round punching through the skirts. The Invy vehicle bounced backwards and settled on the ground, but the plasma cannon started to rotate in their direction.

Dash yelled at the driver to back up, but the gunner yelled, "HOLD!" even as Ibson raced to load the gun. The commander was tempted to kick Lehmkuhl in the head for countermanding her order, but settled on triggering the fifty caliber from her position, hoping the tracer fire and impacts would distract the Invy gunner.

With a HISS CRACK and a charge of static, the plasma bolt scored the top of the turret, melting a groove and overloading the active camouflage. Lehmkuhl fired a second later, the sabot arching out and crashing through the engine of the Invy tank, a small spark followed by an explosion that was so bright it shone through the metal.

Ibson turned to load another sabot round, but Dash shouted, "HEAT, APC, FROM MY POSITION!" Two seconds later Ibson yelled, "UP!" and the commander fired, knocking out an Invy armored personnel carrier that had been crossing the runway.

"All Rifles, general advance," came over the radio, and Banks, listening in, didn't wait for the order. She applied full torque to the drive wheels, and Bad Bitch charged forward, main gun swinging to and fro, searching for targets. On her left *Orca* and *Selchie* followed, barely visible, but *Balrog* was silent and still, a smoking wreck, and *Suzie Q* still burned like a blowtorch.

From the sky, orbital rods began to pound all around the Seattle area, but the radio distractions seemed to be working. For some reason, no one at the base was adjusting fire onto their attack, and Dash was grateful for it. Lehmkuhl let off a snap shot at an Invy tank trying to maneuver west towards the mechanized infantry, who they must have sighted. The Invy's turret bounced upward a foot then settled back, and it crashed, immobile, into the side if a building. The gunner swept the Invy with the coax as they drove past, and *Orca* took out another a kilometer away, blowtorch. Artillery rained down on the base, cratering the runway and shattering the control tower, starting fires.

On her heads up display, targets marked by the infantry as they attacked started to appear as red icons, but Dash ignored them. The display then lit up with a live video feed from a UAV launched in the air from the artillery positions. It only lasted for fifteen seconds before a plasma bolt swept it from the sky, but it was enough to see the hot spots of the three remaining Invy tanks, clustered around the corner of the control tower, shielded from direct artillery fire by the building. Someone was going to have to dig them out. To the left were a ragged line of infantry, Wolverines who, despite the surprise and ferocity of the attack, were dug in and hammering effective shots at the human dismounts.

"Orca," she called over the radio, "go help the dismounts." Her captain was a smear of jelly inside the belly of *Balrog*, so Dash was now in command of the three element unit. "Selchie, I'm going to make a thunder run past their position to get their attention. You come in right behind me, make it quick and make it count."

"You got it," came back immediately, and Dash switched over to the intercom.

"Terry, how fast can you make the bitch go?" she asked the driver.

"No idea, but we're gonna find out!" responded PFC Banks. Locked in her driver's coffin, she had no way of knowing that eight of her friends were dead.

"Punch it, then!"

The seventy ton Abrams, driven by antimatter hellfire, leapt forward, and the turret struggled to keep up with Lehmkuhl's fixed gaze at the corner of the building, rotating as they accelerated forward. When they hit the opening, crossing in front of the three waiting Invy tanks, *Bad Bitch* was going almost ninety miles an hour, the tracks threatening to fly apart at the slightest deviation from a straight line. The first two Invy tanks didn't have the reaction time to fire at her as she sped past, but the third let go just as *Bad Bitch's* cannon fired point blank into it.

Chapter 78

The Invy tank exploded in a thunderous roar, shoving the other two off to one side, but not before the plasma bolt hit *Bad Bitch* in her forward skirt. Her left track exploded in a shower of glowing steel fragments, and the plasma continued though the hull, cutting Terry Banks' legs off at the knees before exiting out the other side.

The tank skidded sideways, losing momentum and power at the same time, and all three of the crew were thrown forward. Dash smashed her face into the commander's sight, cracking the HUD display and knocking her senseless. She crumpled and slid off her seat, on top of Dizzy.

The gunner has seen the shit coming, and leaned into the wall of the tank at the last second, crushing her against it but not injuring her. She was hurt more by Dash falling on her than anything else. In the adrenaline rush, she at first didn't notice the large piece of heavy duty commo wire sticking out of her abdomen, but when she did, the gunner went pale with shock. Then she bit down hard on her lip, drawing blood, and willed the injury out of her mind.

"Gimme, gimme a SITREP…" muttered Dash, but then she followed it with a mumbled, "Johnson, I need a charge five and level that damn gun…" Lehmkuhl knew that she was someplace else, some other when else, and useless. She gently moved her boss aside, trying to ignore the screams coming from the trapped driver.

"Jamie, reload Sabot and poke your head out, tell me what's going on!" she hissed urgently, and the Canadian shook his head to clear it. He manually slid the ammo doors back and loaded a sabot round, muttered UP!, then carefully lifted his hatch a few inches. All the sensors were dead, and it was back to the human eye.

"Jesus! All three Invy are done, *Selchie's* ' blown all to hell, and holy shit, there's one more maneuvering around the wrecks! And I think that's *Orca* burning on the other side! Fuckers' going after the infantry, he's going to eat them for lunch!" The stress and smoke made his voice harsh.

"Get down here and crank the turret!" she yelled, flipping her sight over to manual and pressing her face to it.

The big Canadian slid back down and grabbed at the manual traverse, grunting as he furiously spun the wheel. The compartment was filling up with smoke, but Bank's screams stopped abruptly. They were followed a moment later by the muffled bark of a pistol shot, and Ibson squeezed his eyes shut as he worked. *Goodbye, Terry,* he thought.

"Faster, dammit!" The loader didn't answer Lehmkuhl; his arm was growing tired and he was close to passing out from the fumes. The red emergency lighting and smoke was turning the place into a vision of hell. Suddenly an automated female voice began to blare, "REACTOR CRITICAL, REACTOR CRITICAL" in a flat, dispassionate tone.

Unaware of the puddle of blood growing on the floor beneath her, or not caring, Dizzy Lehmkuhl watched the side skirts of the enemy tank creep into her vision. Closer... closer, and the world began to fade to black around the edges of her vision. Good enough, she thought, and squeezed the trigger.

The 120mm gun jumped backwards, the Invy tank seemed to spin sideways, then a shower of sparks from the main hull, and it settled down, lifeless and smoking. The gunner slumped forward over her sight, then rolled against the breech and lay still.

Corporal Ibson reached down, grabbed Sergeant Dash by the deadman's strap on the back of her coveralls, and heaved. Her slight frame rose up, and he shoved her out of the loader's hatch. Then he grabbed Lehmkuhl around the waist, and manhandled her up, appalled by the amount of blood soaking the front of her uniform.

"Come on, Dizzy, stay with me!" he muttered, trying to get her dead weight out, when a pair of hands reached in and grabbed at her body and pulled her through. Brass from his own 240B machine gun showered down through the open hatch, but he couldn't hear the shots over the screeching of the warning system. '

He pulled himself out, to see two crew men from *Selchie,* one manning the gun, hammering shots at distant enemy infantry. The other was helping Sergeant Dash stumble away towards the other side of the runway. Ibson hit the other man in the shoulder to let him know he was out, but, caught up in the madness of battle, he was ignored. The loader grabbed at him, but a plasma bolt hit the *Selchie* and blew his head off, showering Ibson with superheated blood. The former cop picked up Lehmkuhl's body gently in his arms, slid down the side of *Bad Bitch*, and ran.

What a hell of a way to go! thought *Bad Bitch*, and managed to wait fifteen more seconds, until the Invy infantry had swarmed around her. Then she erupted in a flash of light as the antimatter containment module ruptured, and if a tank had a soul, she joined her friends on Fiddlers' Green.

Chapter 77

It's one thing to face a battle with seventy tons of metal around you. It's a whole different experience to have nothing between you and a hissing bolt of plasma but a few layers of Kevlar and nylon.

Ibson barely made it the edge of the runway with Lehmkuhl when their world was filled with unholy light, and a crushing wave knocked her out of his arms, throwing them both down into the ditch. Then there was deafening silence, punctuated only with the sounds of ammunition cooking off.

"Gotta get back in the fight! Goddamned chinks are ever what go!" yelled Dash, making no sense, and she started to stand up, then stumbled. The crewman from *Selchie* pulled her back down, and laid on top of her to stop her from struggling.

Ibson ignored her for the moment, ripping at the Velcro of Lehmkuhl's vest, then unzipping her coveralls all the way down to her waist. The piece of braided wire, quarter of an inch thick, had slipped under the vest, punched through the tough nylon, and under her ribs. Her whole front was soaked with blood, her belly swollen with internal bleeding, and she looked deathly pale in the glow of the burning control tower.

"Come on, Dizzy, don't do this to me!' he muttered, and felt for a pulse. It was there, but really weak and erratic. He lifted her eyelid and saw that her pupils had rolled upwards, barely showing. Not fucking good. He wrapped a compression bandage around her waist, covering the wound, and elevated her legs. Then he turned to the other man who was dealing with Sergeant Dash, and said, "Can you keep her down?"

"I dunno, dude, she's really out of it. Keeps babbling about killing Chinese."

"OK, I'll be right back," said Ibson, and he stood, glanced around, and ran across the runway. Plasma fire started from another building a hundred meters away, tracking towards him, and then a heavier, automatic weapon chased after the Canadian, making him run faster than he thought he ever could in his life. One almost clipped his boot as he dove behind the smoking wreck of the *Selchie,* and he paused a moment to catch his breath as plasma arced and spit off the hull.

The tank had died with her gun pointing directly at an Invy tank, the turret turned sideways. He knew the soldier helping Dash was *Selchie's* loader, and he had recognized the one killed at the machine gun as her commander. The loader and gunner had probably died inside the turret, but as he looked up, he saw the commander's hatch was open.

Counting out loud, when he reached three, he ran around the side of the tank, grabbed a rail, and vaulted up onto the hull. Before the Invy could zero in on him, Ibson slipped in face first through the hatch, landing on the commander's seat upside down.

The smoke immediately made him start coughing; the emergency red lighting, smell of charred flesh and fried blood made the place seem like some level of Dante's inferno. The loader sat in her seat, missing her bottom half, eyes wide open and staring. The gunner, who had been a good friend of his, slowly cooked as hydraulic fluid dripped onto his mangled body, feeding a small fire. Ibson tried to breathe, but the smell of roasted human flesh overcame him, and he threw up violently. Struggling to turn himself upright, his hands found the medkit he was looking for, unsnapped it from the wall, and he weakly pulled himself out of the hatch, rolled over, and fell the ten feet to the pavement.

He landed on his arm, and there was a sickening SNAP at his wrist, but the tanker gritted his teeth and stood up, slinging the medkit across his body, and tried to peek out around the right side of the tank. Return fire hammered at him so fast he almost lost this head; the Wolverines had zeroed on him, waiting for him to come back. He was stuck, and Dizzy needed him, ASAP.

Screw it. Ibson launched himself out onto the runway, running even faster than he had before. Halfway across, he fell flat, and a burst of fire sheeted over him, the heavy machinegun having waited for him. In a flash, he stood back up and ran again, diving into the ditch and screaming with pain as he slid down the slope.

"Help me!" he yelled, trying to open the medkit one handed. The other soldier made a quick decision, got up of Dash, and helped Ibson open the medkit. Before Dash could get up again, the soldier grabbed a shot of morphine and went back to the disoriented Jamaican.

Ibson quickly found the package of nanos, jabbed the button marked "INTERNAL BLEEDING", waited two seconds, opened it, then jabbed the needle directly into Lehmkuhl's abdomen. She quickly started to convulse, then went rigid, breath heaving in and out. There was one more thing he could do; and he quickly slipped an IV into her veins, which were in danger of collapsing, getting the needle in after three tries, and squeezed the plasma into her until the bag was empty.

Next was an orange pen flare that shot a hundred feet up into the air, calling for a Medevac. Ibson had no idea how the rest of the battle was going; heavy automatic weapons fire and plasma cracks sounded in the distance, but the ones that had been shooting at him on the runway had grown quiet. Too quiet.

A suggestion of movement at the far end of the ditch in the dim moonlight drew his attention, and he hissed a warning to the other soldier, whose name he couldn't remember. They both drew their pistols, and Ibson laid down in front of Lehmkuhl, shielding her body with his. The movement resolved into a squad of Wolverines, who approached them quietly, a six of them led by a Dragon. Half the lesser Invy had their ripper claws extended, and the Dragon leaked blood all over its gold armor, but smiled with razor sharp teeth.

Ibson and the soldier nodded to each other, and raised their pistols. They were dead men, but they knew they had beaten the Invy if the Dragon was fleeing the Command Center. Fuck it. They had won. It was kind of bitter sweet, to have come so far, but …

Thirty tons of Bradley Fighting Vehicle crashed over the side of the ditch and into the Invy squad, knocking them down like bowling pins. The driver ground the tracks back and forth, spinning the vehicle first one way then the next, grinding the stunned Invy into a red paste of patches of skin, snapped bones, and raw meat.

One of the Wolverines had escaped the collision, and the two men emptied their pistols into it from ten meters away, firing until their slides locked back. The Bradley stopped, and the turret rotated, hammering out thunderous three round bursts even as the back ramp slammed down. Before it did, Ibson saw a crude green and black painting of a long necked animal spitting plasma, and knew it was one of Alpha Companies' Brads, nicknamed *Attack Llama*. The infantry squad leader directed two of his men to help the wounded to the track; they quickly strapped Lehmkuhl onto a stretcher and carried her inside.

The rest joined the main gun in firing towards the buildings, then at some unseen signal, the firing stopped, and they all dashed back into the track. As the ramp whirred up, they were thrown violently to one side, and then the Brad started back down the runway towards the impromptu Aide Station a mile away. One man struggled to strap Dash into a seatbelt, and she fought wildly, despite the morphine, then slumped and lay still, a spray of blood leaking out of her nose. The man put his fingers to her neck, searching for a pulse, looked at his NCO, and shook his head.

In the battle lighting, Ibson could see that every man there, even the ones who had dismounted and continued fighting, was badly wounded or burned. The squad leader leaned over and yelled in Ibsons' ear, "You guys really saved our asses! Where's the rest of the tank crews?"

The Canadian said nothing in answer, just reached over and held Lehmkuhl's bloody, slightly warm hand in his. Then he put his other hand over his face, and great, wracking sobs convulsed his body. The infantryman next to him put his arm around Ibson's neck, and the tanker laid his head on his shoulder, still bleeding silent tears.

No one said anything for the rest of the short ride.

Part VI

"Scouts Out"

Invy Airfield, outside the ruins of Washington, D.C.

I just can't get it clear in my head, Jess. He was so full of living, you know? He ran a franchise on it. Now there's nothing. And here I am trying to put sense to it, when I know there isn't any.

~ *"Mad" Max Rockatansky*

Chapter 78

The exhausted soldiers of Scout Team One huddled behind the shattered remnants of what looked to be the remains of an F-35, eleven years of rust and weather having reduced the wreck to a skeleton. It had been fifteen minutes since the shuttle had taken off, fifteen minutes of hell that seemed to last a thousand years. They had accomplished their mission, getting a pilot onto an Invy shuttle so she could steal it, but now, well there seemed no way out.

"Give me an up!" shouted Master Sergeant Agostine, over the hiss and crack of plasma bolts seeking their position. The Invy were pissed, no doubt, and making it known. It almost drowned out the deeper rumblings of the attack happening on the far side of the base.

Each of the team gave him a thumbs up, except for Zivcovic and Yassir, who had both crawled up on the tilted wing with their sniper rifles. "We're good!" shouted Redshirt, who was spotting for them, but he didn't take his eyes off his binos. He called out targets, and each of the snipers fired in an alternating rhythm, rolling back down as return fire erupted around them.

"Another two APC's" said Redshirt, his words punctuated by the deep WHAM WHAM WHAM as a vehicle mounted cannon probed the wreck. On either side lay a hundred meters of open ground between them and the next cover.

"Shit shit shit," muttered Agostine. "Jones, get on the radio, and get us some fucking HELP!" said the team leader, stress obvious in his voice. "Mortars, Javelins, whatever they can do." Their own launcher unit lay shattered on the weedy tarmac, in the hands of Staff Sergeant Boyd, whose headless body still twitched.

They had completed their mission, gotten the pilot to the Invy shuttle and covered the launch, but everything had gone to shit after that. The garrison's reaction time had been faster than planned, and the team had found their exit route blocked by a squad of Wolverines manning crew served weapons. Now, in full daylight, the enemy seemed to have enough forces to deal with both the diversionary attack AND go after the scouts.

A drone buzzed around the corner of the wrecked aircraft, its antigrav pulsers whining, and Jones dropped the handmic, grabbed up the auto shotgun, and hammered away at it, three quick shots that sent high velocity birdshot at the small craft. It wobbled, recovered, and sped away. The big NCO turned back to the radio, calling angrily into it.

"Lost Boys, this is Foehammer, one minute out, mark targets, over," came crackling over the radio. Jones flipped through the signals book taped to his arm, looking for who the call sign belonged to.

"Air Force, Nick, coming in hot, needs to mark target."

The Scout team leader scrambled to remember how to get air support on target; it had been more than a decade. "Reynolds, put smoke on those bastards, now!" said Agostine, but she was moving before he said it, lining up her M-320 to get the range, even as she fumbled for a 40mm smoke round. This was her first taste of a full on engagement, and her hands were shaking like a leaf as she slid the round in.

With a hollow TONK the grenade arched upward, landed, and started to spew orange smoke in front of the armor, even as their ramps dropped down and Wolverines started to claw from the back. Their squat forms were quickly obscured as the orange mist enveloped them, but plasma carbine bolts started to hammer into the F-35 wreckage.

"Foehammer, we are approximately one zero zero meters forty degrees magnetic of the target, along the runway, target marked with orange smoke, over."

"I COPY ONE ZERO ZERO FORTY, ORANGE SMOKE!" came back the strained voice of the pilot as she fought against G forces and the shaking of her fifty year old plane. *"Twenty seconds, I can only give you one pass, guns and cluster!"*

"FRIENDLY CAS IN FIFTEEN!' yelled Jones, and everyone huddled on the ground, trying to weld themselves to the tarmac. A hundred meters was way within the danger close for this type of work. Only Agostine stood, not caring. He watched the black dot in the sky resolve itself in the Devils Cross. Even as he looked, the nose of the plane disappeared in a blaze of light.

BRRRRRRRRRRRRRRRRRRRRRRRRRRRRRRRRRRRRRRR RRRRTTTTTTTTTTTTTTTTTTTTTTTTTTTTTT came the report, as the plane seemed to stagger in air, 30mm depleted uranium rounds the size of his hand reaching out and plowing into the APC's. One exploded in a thunderous BANG that lifted the entire armored shell into the sky, and the other was blown sideways, fire jetting out of blown hatches.

The A-10 rocketed overhead, and two shapes fell from its wings, then burst open, showering what was left of the Wolverines with hundreds of grenade sized bomblets. Their explosions seemed almost anticlimactic after the APC detonation.

"OK," said Agostine, a grim smile on his face as the beautiful plane arched upward, turned over, and dove at the Invy positions on the other side of the base, where the Main Force units were still attacking. "OK," he said again, almost to himself, "let's get the hell out of here."

"Nick, are you crying?" asked Zivcovic and he bandaged a burn on his arm. "You are pussy."

"Suck it, you Serbian gangster," he answered back. "It's beautiful. Goddamned beautiful."

Chapter 79

"Lost Boys Six, this is Shiva Six, over," crackled the radio.

Jones handed the radio over to Agostine with a look of glee on his face, and he took it with a murderous glare. "This is Lost Boys, go," he answered abruptly.

"Stand by for extraction, priority mission. Shiva out."

The team leader looked at the radio, then put the hand mike down in disgust. He just wanted the day to be over, and the sun had barely come up. Whatever, he thought, he was tired way down deep. Agostine glanced at the headless body of Staff Sergeant Boyd, and made another black mark on his soul.

They trudged wearily towards the coordinates the pilots gave them as the base burned behind them, sliding down into a ravine just big enough to clear the rotors of a Blackhawk, but only just. Between them, Zivcovic and Jones carried the heavy bag containing Boyd's body. No one said anything; they were exhausted from the fight and the death of one of their team. The soldiers waited almost an hour, each lost in their thoughts; though each wanted to sleep, none could.

Eventually, with a whirr of stealthed rotors, the MH-60C settled to the ground just long enough for the team to climb aboard. They buckled in, knowing what would come next; hanging out of helicopters with your feet dangling in the breeze was a thing of the past. The Sikorski rose, pivoted, and launched itself northwards, a bare ten feet off the ground. The next fifteen minutes was dizzying, gut wrenching trip, until they cleared the nearest Invy base that might have line of sight on them.

As they passed through the ruins of Washington's suburbs, gaining some altitude to clear some of the bigger buildings, Agostine plugged his headset into the intercom and asked the crew chief what the big picture was.

"Your bird got away, good job on that. We took the station, but the Invy scrambled the core, and we have no control over it," he answered, eyes moving between the ground and the sky, looking for threats.

"What about the rest?" There had been four.

The crew chief spit some tobacco juice out, and Redshirt leaned over, slapped him on the leg. The chief handed him a precious can of Skoal and the Navajo nodded gratefully, passing it around to the team. "Well," said the crewman, "rumor control has it that the Brits lost their guys when their target reactor went critical. The Japs lost their shuttle to defensive fire from Orbital Three, so it's still up there, blew the crap out of a lot of the West Coast."

"It was a mistake to send only one shuttle," answered Agostine. They were passing over the Potomac, choked with debris, and, looking out, the Scout Team Leader could the myriad of round ponds, filled in craters from orbital strikes.

"Probably. But no one gives a shit what we think, Sarge," answered the chief. "Hang on!" he said, and gripped the side of the helo as they dipped low, flared, and came in for a landing. The rotor wash threw up clouds of trash and dust, making everyone cough. Agostine unplugged, and the crew chief made a circling motion, asking them to pull security. The team spilled out, fanning out in a 360 degree arc.

"Anyone here can climb a pole?" asked the pilot, looking around at the decrepit site. There were piles of windblown trash and debris at the base of the statue.

"Tiffany, you're the lightest, go," said Agostine, and the sniper got up, walked over to the statue, and started climbing, five fifty cord gripped in her teeth. She reached the rusty pulley on top of the pole, hanging from her knees and one arm, and slipped the light green paracord into the wheel. Reynolds fed the cord through until it reached the ground, then shimmied back down.

The pilot reached back into the helo and took out two packages, one red white and blue, the other dark blue and gold. The Chief tied a heavier rope to the line, snapped a flag to it, ran it up a little, and then snapped the other underneath it. Then he pulled, making the rusty pulley squeal as he raised it.

The idling helo made the flags snap in the wind, and above the blue and gold of the Confederated Earth Forces, the Star and Stripes caught the morning sun. Beneath it, the four Marines, forever frozen in time, reached to lift it higher.

Nick Agostine turned from scanning for targets just as the American flag unraveled to full length. When he saw it, he felt a tightness grow in his chest, a pain that was unbearable. So many lost, and Brit would never see this day. He started to cry, silent tears that rolled down through the dirt and dust on his face, spilling onto his rifle. *Why?* he asked himself. She had died only a few weeks ago, so close to this day. Cut down by an Invy plasma bolt, rescuing that bastard General Warren. They had been so close to being able to live a life together, and there was so much left unsaid. Her red hair and ice blue eyes haunted him, and he could almost hear her laugh at him and his seriousness.

"This is some cheesy shit, no?" said Zivcovic, interrupting his thoughts. "Why no camera, to film propaganda bullshit?"

"Hey Ahmed, how do you say asshole in Arabic?" said Doc.

"I think the word is 'Al-ziv-covic-a', but I am not sure," he grinned, and the Serb gave him the finger.

Behind them, the rotors started to increase in volume, and one by one, they climbed back into the helo, Agostine the last aboard. He looked back one more time as they rose up in the air, and the nose tilted forward. He held up his hand to block out the sun, and watched as the flag disappeared into the distance.

When they touched down at Raven Rock, Colonel Singh was impatiently waiting for them. She motioned for Agostine and Hamilton to follow her, and entered a small conference room. General Dalpe, looking haggard after a night of no sleep, sat in a chair at the head of a small table. He dismissed his Chief of Staff, and the man glanced at the two scouts as he left.

"Gentlemen, how familiar are you with Long Island?"

"New York?" asked Agostine. "I grew up there, Farmingdale."

"I've been, quite a few times before the war," said Hamilton. "Used to run our bikes along the Jones Beach causeway."

"Well, there's an Invy base near Calverton that they are using as a sort of POW camp. The old Brookhaven research facility; they have a bunch of scientists that have either gone over to them, or are being compelled to work for them. For the long term battle, we are going to need those men and women."

"So," said Agostine, glancing at Singh, who looked back at him stonily, "you want us to scout it? Get the layout for a Main Force attack?"

Dalpe shook his head. "No," he said tiredly, "we need you to take it."

Chapter 80

"Very funny," said the team chief, but neither Dalpe nor Singh laughed.

When he saw the looks on their faces, Agostine put his hands down flat on the table, and said emphatically, "No."

The General bristled at that, starting to say something, but Singh raised her hand to calm him. "Nick," she said, "I wouldn't sign off on this if I didn't think we could do it."

"We? I've got seven people on my team, and, yeah, we're the best, but that's half a dozen against, what, a company of Wolverines?"

Dalpe interrupted, and said, "Master Sergeant, these people are going to be critical to the war effort. Scout Team Four reconned the area last year; the fighting in the City will have drawn off all their armor. You'll be facing the slackers they left behind."

Agostine sneered at that. "Slackers, my ass. When was the last time YOU faced a Wolverine? I'll listen to Rachel, you can fuck off for all I care …. Sir."

Infuriated, the General rose up out of his chair. Agostine stood also, but Hamilton grabbed him in a bear hug, holding him back. "Nick, let it go!" he said to him, then nodded to Singh. "We'll do it, just give us enough time to get our shit together." Agostine shook him off, looked at Dalpe, and walked out of the room, not waiting to be dismissed.

Rachel Singh caught up with him in the hallway, grabbed his arm, and stopped him. "What the HELL was that?" she said angrily. "Do you think I'm just going to send you on a suicide mission?"

"Honestly?" he shot back, "I don't know anymore. You sent us chasing after Warren, and that got Brit killed!"

"So that's what this is about?"

"That, and other things. Like Boyd coming back headless this morning. And how many of my soldiers are going to die today on this mission?"

She slapped him, directly across the face, and he reeled backward, more in shock than at the force of the blow. "Damn you!" she shouted, not caring who heard. "Those were MY soldiers too! Do you know WHY I am sending in your team and not Team Four? Because THEY are all dead! And Team Seven, and Team Two! All dead on MY ORDERS!"

She stormed away, and Agostine stood there, stunned. Hamilton came up, and said, "Way to go, Nick," then brushed past him.

He followed them down the corridor to the team room, where the guys were cleaning weapons and gear. Hamilton and Singh waited for him to come up, but neither said anything. Agostine took a deep breath, let it out, and said simply, "Sorry." Then he opened the door and went in.

Inside, he looked at each one there. Jones, Zivcovic, Reynolds, Redshirt, Yassir, each in turn. How many of them were going to be back here tomorrow? Never mind, he told himself. They were soldiers, and knew what they in for. So he told himself.

"Listen up, we have another mission. It's going to be tough, and dangerous. I'm not asking for volunteers; you're all going because we can't afford to not have you with us, each of you is an integral part of the team. Having said that, I'm going to let Colonel Singh do the mission brief."

She looked at him, then stepped up, placing a holojector on the table. A map lit up, showing a compound in three dimensions. There was a series of buildings on what looked like a college campus, and, as she tilted it, they saw an unusual ring shaped land formation.

"This was Brookhaven National Laboratory. The Invy are using it as a research facility, into both human genetics and particle physics. Why both in one place, we don't know, but it is what it is. Our mission," eyes went up at the use of the word 'our', "will be to secure the barracks area here," she said, pointing to a three story structure.

"Once we secure it," she continued, "we will take as many of the scientists with us that we can, and exfil by air."

Agostine stepped up and said, "Since you keep saying we, I assume you're going with us."

"Yes." she answered, "you're short on personnel."

"That's fine, but tactical control of the team is on me. If you go, you're going as a shooter. Understood?"

She nodded, and continued, "We will have some help on the ground. A CEF pathfinder team went in early this morning by boat from New Haven, they will have eyes on the target, and will assist in the raid. They spent the last few weeks scouting the target, and know it well. Insertion will be on foot from an LZ due south. Once the captives are secured, your ride, a CV-22 Osprey, will do the pickup. From there, you will exfil by foot north to submarine pickup on Long Island Sound, then to our Main Force base in New Haven."

There was silence in the room for a long moment, then Zivcovic said, "Is bullshit."

"Excuse me?" said Singh, who hadn't often worked with the Serb and wasn't used to his brusque manner.

"I say, is bullshit. You are going to get plane shot down and all captives killed. A plasma bolt will take the entire aircraft down. "

It was a flaw in their plan, and she knew it. One she had already argued with Dalpe about, but he had insisted. The man's nerves were ragged, and she knew not to push it. What happened on the ground would stay on the ground. "If anyone has any other suggestions, by all means, I'm open to them."

"First off, bring the pilots in here to help us plan," said Agostine. "Colonel, I knew you're being handed a shit sandwich by higher, and you have just as much experience planning as any of us do, so we can use your help, but you can't do it alone." It was his way of trying to make up with her, and she felt the knot in her stomach loosen a little.

"Having said that, we're going to come up with a plan, and General Dalpe is going to have to accept it. Your job will be to run interference for us, and keep him off our back."

"Nick," she said, "he has a war to run. If we tell him we can handle the mission, he'll run with that and let us do our thing."

"OK then," he said, glancing at his watch. "It's zero eight hundred now." He stopped at that. Had it really only been two hours since they had been engaged in the fight with the Invy?

Agostine continued, planning backwards, "It's about two hour flight, assuming we need to swing south or north of the City. We are going to want to hit the place at dusk, to make sure the majority of POW's are back at their barracks, which is around six thirty, so assuming we have an hour's march to the attack site, five thirty, four thirty, three thirty, wheels up is at fifteen hundred. You all have four hours to get some sleep and finish taking care of your weapons and supplies. We're going to wargame the shit out of this and do a sandbox at thirteen hundred."

Redshirt raised his hand and asked, "Why not wait for later? Like, zero three or something?"

"Good question," said Singh. "Big picture, we feel that, if things aren't going well for the Invy, they will consolidate and pull south below thirty degrees. That means they're going to slaughter every captive they have."

"Why are we walking out?" asked Reynolds.

"Because we're expendable. No offense, but eight of us on the bird means eight less scientists that we don't take with us."

Chapter 81

Ziv slept, or pretended to. Ahmed prayed silently. Red sat working quietly on a carving. Reynolds watched Ziv. Hamilton read a medical book on his Kindle. Jones ate MRE after MRE. Singh watched out the window as the landscape of Connecticut slipped by. It was interesting to see how they each reacted to the stress of the upcoming mission; yet they were calmer than most. What was that old quote from World War Two? The only way to deal with combat was to accept that you were already dead.

Eight men and women, thought Agostine, to take on from maybe a dozen to, crap, several dozen Wolverines and Dragons. A UAV flight had confirmed, before it was shot out of the sky, that the majority of the garrison had driven westward on the Long Island Expressway, heading for the fighting in New York City. That had turned into a meat grinder, with both forces pushing in troops, but the CEF had the advantage, having spent the last decade turning the buildings of Manhattan into a death trap for armored vehicles. None of the Scout's business, though.

Word had come late in the day that the last orbital had been destroyed by a Japanese assault team, led by a Major Ikeda. Agostine had met the man several years before, on an intel operation to check out the Invy cities, and liked and respected him. Good for them, he thought, and good for us. No more orbital threat.

Of the war in space, well, they had heard nothing. Or, if they had, no one was sending it down to the mushrooms of the individual soldiers. Kept in the dark and fed shit, he mused. One thing he knew for sure, that General Warren was alive and somehow plugged into the net. That rumor had been all over the base. It was a good thing to know, because, when the war was over, Nick was going to kill him. With a plasma rifle, to the gut. So he could die the way Brit had.

"Hey!" said Zivcovic to Jones, "do you think we are getting back in time go to Raver Rock? We are war heroes now! Maybe get some ass."

"Shee-it, why you gotta be so rude to Reynolds? You got a fine girl there, Ziv."

Reynolds started to splutter, "WE AREN'T …!" but Jones just laughed.

"What is Raver Rock?" asked Singh, bewilderment on her face.

"Don't tell her, Nick, she's an officer," said Jones, gleefully. "If you do, the E-4 mafia is gonna put out a hit on you!"

"I'm not scared of what they can do to me," he answered with a grin.

"It's what they WON'T do FOR you anymore," laughed Doc Hamilton.

Singh was totally lost, and her confusion only exacerbated their mirth. To put her out of her misery, Agostine said, "Raver Rock is a sort of, um, dance club, run by a certain, ah, rank of enlisted soldier, aided and abetted by certain higher ranking NCO's. It moves from room to room in the base."

"Seriously?" she asked. "I've never even heard of this. What is the 'E-4 mafia'?"

"It's… something you have to experience. Like the WPPA."

"The what?" she asked, even more confused.

"West Point Protective Association!" laughed Jones. "How you ring knockers look out for each other."

Singh smiled and said, "No academy for me, I was ROTC!"

"Good thing, else we might have to throw you off the plane," said Ahmed, getting into the spirit of things.

"But seriously, what is the E-4 mafia?" she asked again.

"As the only actual E-4 here, I will tell you, but the spirit of my ancestors tell me I have to kill you," said Redshirt. "After the mission, of course, Ma'am."

"Of course!" she smiled back at him.

"Well, many moons ago …" he began.

"Cut the Indian bullshit, I know you were studying molecular biology at Harvard when the invasion happened."

The Navajo smiled, and continued, "Well, a long time ago, Baron Von Steuben created a special rank called 'Corporal', the lowest rank that has any power, and lo, the privates did wail and complain."

"Like they do," interjected Hamilton.

Redshirt ignored him, and continued, "And eventually, the gods of war created a rank called 'Specialist', which was liken unto a Corporal, with all the knowledge but no power. So the Specialists did form a secret society, called the "E-4 mafia" to watch over the junior enlisted, and to protect them all from abuses of power. Many is the leader who has regretted crossing them, even unto this day."

"And this 'mafia' still exists? Even after the Invasion?" asked Singh.

"They have only grown more powerful, supposedly. Remember, this is only a legend, Ma'am. But, anything is possible. In fact, we are pretty sure the Wolverines have their own."

At that moment, the Osprey dove down and swerved left, making them all grab onto their harnesses. *"Sorry about that,"* came the pilot's voice over the intercom. *"Random plasma fire from the fight for the City."*

The maneuver brought back a little soberness, and no one had much to say after that. At five minutes out, a red light started flashing inside the cabin, and they each said their own prayers, and looked to their equipment. The landing was anticlimactic, setting down in a deserted parking lot, surrounded by derelict cars and a wrecked shopping center.

Glass crunched under boots as the team filed out, while the Osprey crew erected a camouflage net over the VTOL. Each soldier carried an enormous burden, over a hundred pounds of weapons, ammo and water.

"This plan better work," said Agostine as he walked next to Singh.

"It's better than my plan, I'll admit it," she said.

"Well, when you put a bunch of experienced people together, you generally do come up with something better. You know that."

"I do." She seemed pensive, and Agostine looked at her with concern, though he was still irritated at her.

"Come on, Rachel, I know my head isn't into the game, but I know why," he said. "You could have come up with a better plan in your sleep."

"Yeah, I could have. A week ago. Now, well, I haven't slept in almost that long. This war… I just want to go home, and I don't have a home anymore."

"Are you going to be an asset or a liability?" She knew what he meant. A liability that would get them killed.

"I'm not going to get anyone killed, if that is what you're asking." She wouldn't look him in the eye when she said it, though.

"Good. Don't, I'd be upset. Or you, either. Thanks for hitting me before." It was his way of a peace offering.

"Sometimes we all need to be slapped back to our senses. You're a good soldier, Nick, but I hope you can put that bleeding heart of yours away." With that, Rachel Singh picked up her pace and left a very worried Master Sergeant walking towards their objective.

Chapter 82

They met the pathfinders a kilometer out, two by two as each section of the team slipped into the hide site. Agostine came in last, along with Doc Hamilton. It was in the basement of a ruined McMansion that smelled of mold and dankness.

"So, down to business," said the first, a small, dark skinned man. He didn't give his name or rank, nor did his partner, but Agostine knew them both to be members of Scout Team 22, which specialized in infiltrating Invy bases and facilities.

The second man lit up a holojector, bright in the basement's darkness. It showed the Brookhaven Campus, with their target building lit in blue, and suspected Invy positions in red. "We spent the last four weeks inside the compound, scouting locations, and this is what we got."

"Four weeks, damn," muttered Jones, and the man smiled in the darkness, but continued on.

"The Invy barracks are here," and a building lit with red. "Air defense here, and here," more red, "and their Command Center here. All their bunkers face outward; we dug a tunnel from the closest safe sewer entrance to this building here."

"All that in four weeks?" asked Reynolds in amazement.

"No," said the first. "We dug the tunnel three years ago. Never know when you're going to need something, right? It was Colonel Singh's idea."

She just looked at Agostine smugly. Plans within plans within plans. That's why she was the Colonel, not him. He'd take her on tactics over strategy any day, though.

"Single watchtower with a sensor ball, here," middle of the camp, "should be easy enough with the Barrett. No watch towers, squad sized Quick Reaction Force, and maybe another dozen Wolverines as guard. Probably less than ten, considering they pulled most of the garrison out to head to the City."

"Pretty lax security for a POW camp," said Red.

"Where are they going to go?" answered the man. "Long Island is a wreck, three million people stuffed into suburbs when the power went out. There probably isn't a soul alive between here and Manhattan."

'Good point," said the Navajo.

"OK, then, plan stays the same, except, well, how big is this tunnel?" asked Agostine.

"About four foot high, maybe three wide," said the first pathfinder, "it was the best we could do with this sandy soil." Everyone looked at Jones; it was obvious that he would never fit. It was going to be a tight squeeze with our equipment and weapons.

"Alrighty then," said J. "I guess I'm on the distraction team instead of Red?"

"Not instead of," Agostine answered. "In addition to. We were originally going to go for a sniper attack, right? Well, now we're just going to add bang to the buck. Take all of AT-4's and blow the shit out of the buildings on the north side."

"Will that leave us enough people to handle the POWs?" asked Zivcovic.

"Ahmed and these two guys. Doc, you, me and Colonel Singh will do the entry, and each of the others will line twenty meters with a light, back to the LZ. Rachel, sorry, I mean Colonel, you take the rear when we rush the barracks. Ahmed, your target is the sensor." He had wanted her to stay out of it, escort the prisoners, but honestly he trusted Ahmed to deal with an emergency more than her, in her tired state.

"And the Air Defense?" she asked.

"We've got that wired, there's an EMP mine buried five meters from each, low charge. Too tricky to get explosives directly onto the guns," said the second pathfinder.

"OK, then. Team two," said Agostine, meaning Jones, Red and Reynolds, "move out. We'll give you an hour to get into position. Watch out for drones if you can, and make sure you drink water. You know what the camo suits can do to you."

They didn't say anything, just made their way out of the entrance to the basement. Along the way, each team member handed Jones an AT-4, until he carried six of the tubes in addition to the captured Invy plasma anti-tank gun.

"Can you handle that?" asked Red, pushing down hard on Jones' pack. The big man shrugged him off, smiled, then easily pushed the small Navajo aside.

"The rest of you, take ten to get whatever PCI's you need to do. Colonel, can I talk to you for a minute?" She didn't say anything, just took the stairs up to the ruined first floor, disappearing as she activated her camo suit. Agostine did the same, following her up.

"Rachel, I have a question for you, and I wanted to ask you away from everyone else, in case you didn't want to be seen giving the order," said the Master Sergeant.

"You don't have to ask," his boss answered. "Any POW's that don't want to go with you, you execute. We can only take thirty max anyway, and the Pathfinders estimate fifty or more."

"That's pretty harsh," he said. "And you never brought that up in the mission brief."

"The Invy are going to execute and eat the ones we leave anyway, not necessarily in that order, Nick. It's a mercy, really. And I have my orders, just like you do."

"It's not right, Rachel," he said, face stony.

She shook her head, and said, "You have no problem with the ODA's executing collaborators."

"They know who is a shitbag and who isn't, they've been scoping their targets for almost a decade," he shot back.

"You know we don't have time for sorting through who is who. Just grab who you can, maybe the younger ones, but maybe not the healthier looking ones. They're probably actively collaborating in exchange for food and good treatment." To him, it seemed a rehearsed answer, one she had been telling herself over and over.

"How much time on the objective?" he asked, dropping the objections. He would deal with it later.

"Depends on how they react to the diversion. Ten minutes maybe?" she answered.

"OK, that will do. If it looks like opposition is tough, I'm leaving them. I don't have the time to play executioner at the expense of my people. Besides, it isn't right, and you know it." His jaw was firmly set, even though she couldn't see it.

"Master Sergeant," said Colonel Singh, her voice frosty, "I am giving you a direct order to neutralize any scientists that you cannot take with you, or who are not willing to go."

He said nothing in answer for a minute, then said, "No. You'll have to do it yourself. I won't stop you, but I'm tired of killing, and I'm not going to ask my people to do it."

"Are you refusing my order? SERGEANT HAMILTON!" she called.

Doc appeared a moment later, then disappeared as he activated his own camo. "Yes, Ma'am?" he asked, but he had been listening below.

"I am relieving Master Sergeant Agostine of command. You are now in charge," she said simply.

There was silence, then Doc Hamilton said, "It doesn't work that way, Colonel. You wrote the rules yourself. You can fire him all you want once we get back, but out in the field, he's in charge. You're just here as an extra gun, with all due respect."

That wasn't what she had expected, and she looked pissed. "Well, then. I guess I'm going to have to do it myself. Are you going to stop me? Either of you?" She knew that Hamilton had been listening to their conversation.

"Rachel, you don't want that on your soul," said Agostine. "I'll shoot outright collaborators, if we can prove it, but anyone we can't take on the bird, I'll try to get out through Escape and Evasion. The rest of the team can go, and you can send a recovery sub or boat."

"That will get you killed," she said.

"Probably. But better to lose my life than my soul," he answered in a tired voice.

Singh walked away, leaving the matter unsettled.

Chapter 83

The worst part was waiting in the tunnel. It was small, tight, and though they had lined it with rough concrete, there was still a smell of mold and dirt. Each soldier was packed in tight with the one in front, Zivcovic in the lead. Behind him was Agostine and then Hamilton, and each had their hand on the boot of the man in front of him. Singh took up the rear position. They had looked at video taken of the tunnel exit, and a night vision peek at the target building, just across the street.

They knew there was going to be a lot of confusion, and Agostine had put Zivcovic in the lead for that reason. The man just didn't care if a human got in his line of fire, and Agostine feared that he himself would hesitate. He was truly sick of the killing, and he had decided that this was his last mission.

"I have to piss," said Zivcovic, and proceeded to.

"Couldn't you have done that before we crowded in here?" Agostine asked, the strong smell of urine assaulting their noses. There were many situations where the scouts had to crap and piss right where they were, but this wasn't one of those.

"No," the Serb answered simply.

"You're a real asshole sometimes, you know?" said Hamilton.

"Thank you," said Ziv.

They were doing it to mask the tension of waiting, to try and calm racing hearts, though Zivcovic probably had a high heartbeat due to joy at facing battle.

Agostine ordered, "None of your bullshit single combat this time."

"I do what I must do," said Zivcovic, "Honor demands it."

Singh spoke up from the rear, saying, "Sergeant Zivcovic, if you even think about it, I will shoot you in the back of the head. Do you understand me?"

He looked back at her, and she could see his feral grin in the darkness. "You would make a good Serb wife, if you weren't from a lesser people." But he didn't talk back to her about her order. It was weird, thought Agostine, but Zivcovic always listened to her.

They felt, more than heard, a distant explosion, just as their timers reached 18:30, and they waited, one minute, two minutes, three, then Agostine slapped Ziv's shoulder. The Serb moved forward, pushing through the false wall that hid the entrance to the tunnel. It fell forward, and into an empty basement.

Moving swiftly up and into the open, their chameleon suits hiding them in the darkness, they ran towards the barracks. Zivcovic focused straight ahead, Agostine to the right, and Hamilton to the left. In the rear, Singh raised her weapon and scanned the rooftop as they ran. She was the first to fire, stopping to draw a good sight picture at a Wolverine that was looking over the edge, northward. The IR laser settled center mass on the form, and she fired three sabot rounds, one catching it in the shoulder and the next in head, a spray of heat showing in her goggles. She immediately continued scanning the roof and windows, running to catch the rest of the team.

Zivcovic fired his shotgun twice, shattering the hinges on the side, and Agostine grabbed the handle and pulled, letting the Serb peel in through the door. Inside was a long corridor that led to individual rooms; these were where the collaborators lived.

"Cells are on the third floor, let's go!" said Singh, and they ran down the corridor as doors started to open. "CEF! GET BACK IN YOUR ROOMS!" yelled Singh. To emphasize her words, she shot a woman who didn't move fast enough, hammering her back into her doorway. The rest got the message and ducked back inside. Agostine looked at her, but she just looked back coldly.

They took the steps two at a time, Ziv's shotgun booming as a Wolverine came down the stairs. The creature, even though mortally wounded, launched itself at him, and he fired again, the buckshot catching it in the face, shattering its skull. It was the only Invy they encountered going up the stairway. There had been a guard booth inside the door, but it had been empty; they were probably all on the roof, looking at the attack a kilometer away. At the second floor, they kicked in the doorway, took a quick glimpse into it, saw no enemies, and shut it.

"Doc, you and Rachel take the third floor, and start getting the POW's out. Ziv, you and I take the roof. Be careful," he said to his oldest friend, and Hamilton gripped his shoulder, then turned to the door. The Serb ejected all his buckshot rounds, and slipped in slugs made of tungsten.

Agostine and Zivcovic moved slowly up the stairs, weapons pointed straight up. The door to the roof was slightly ajar, and the Team Leader motioned for Ziv to let him see. A quick look showed the dead Wolverine that Singh had shot, and another three manning a heavy weapons platform. They were firing in the general direction of where explosions were still happening.

"Not the brightest, are they?" muttered the Master Sergeant.

"They leave the shitbags on guard duty; all the good ones run towards the battle," answered the Serb with a grin.

Agostine motioned for Ziv to give him his grenades. Why risk a missed shot and return fire? He laid four of the round devices on the step in front of him, removed the rubber bands around the spoons, picked up the first one, and, in quick succession, pulled each pin, flipped off the spoon, and threw it out the door, to skid across the rooftop towards the gun emplacement.

He had just thrown the last one when the first went off, with a CRACK!, followed by the rest. A second after the last blast, the two men charged out the door, firing repeatedly at whatever hotspots showed in their helmet displays, until they expended their magazines.

All three Wolverines were hammered with multiple shots, even though two were already dead. The third managed to get off a bolt from a rifle that burned past Agostine's head, and his helmet display shorted out with the plasma discharge, leaving a clear plastic sheet in front of his face. He slapped the reboot button with one hand while still firing bursts at the creature, even though Ziv had already hammered it with sabot rounds.

"CLEAR!" said Ziv, and Agostine answered "CLEAR!" The two men turned and ran back down the stairs, calling out ahead over the radio so they didn't get shot.

"Nick, we've got seventeen here, but some of them are non-mobile," Hamilton called back.

"Be there in a second," answered Agostine, and he told Zivcovic to guard the stairwell, then slipped in through the third floor doorway, just as pistol shots began to bark.

Chapter 84

"What the hell are you doing?" demanded Agostine.

Rachel Singh put her pistol back in its holster, and ignored him. Four bodies lay on the floor, each shot through the head. A dozen filthy men and women cowered at the end of the hallway, fear on their faces.

"Sergeant Hamilton, you're in charge of the evacuees. Take these, then go with Master Sergeant Agostine down to the first floor and get another dozen, anyway you can, and move them out to the LZ. Sergeant Zivcovic, come with me." She brushed past the stunned Agostine, and Ziv followed her down the stairs. At that moment, Agostine wanted to kill her.

"Nick," said Hamilton, "let's go. There's nothing else to do here."

"Rob, I can't do this shit anymore," he said, and leaned back against the wall, closing his eyes.

The big biker grabbed his friend's arm and shook him. "Listen, brother, you crack on me now, and all these other people are going to die. You can quit later, but I need you right now. Let's go."

The NCO opened his eyes, and Hamilton could see the bleakness in his soul. He stared at a pretty blonde woman with a hole in her forehead and terror on her face, reached down, and closed her eyelids. "OK, let's go."

"You take lead, and I'll move them from the back," said Doc, and they approached the cowering POW's.

"My name is Master Sergeant Agostine, CEF Scouts, and we're here to rescue you," Agostine said, but got no reaction, so he grabbed one man by the arm and shoved him in the direction of the doorway. None of the others moved, and something in Agostine broke.

"GODDAMNIT, MOVE!" he yelled, and fired a burst into the ceiling. They screamed and ran past him, and Agostine pushed his way to the door. As he made his way down the stairs, past the second floor, he could pistol shots and screams. Zivcovic stood in the doorway, but he wasn't shooting anything.

Clenching his teeth in anger at what he had to ignore, the scout cautiously opened the door to the first floor. The body of the woman Singh had killed lay sprawled half in her doorway, but all the others were shut. "COME OUT!" he yelled, "OR WE'RE GOING TO FIRE INTO YOUR ROOMS!"

The doors started opening, mostly men, well fed and decently clothed, stepping out. Collaborators. It disgusted him, but he was sick of the whole thing already. Agostine started grabbing at some of them, women in particular, because he knew what was going to happen to them if they weren't rescued. When he had a dozen, he herded them towards the wrecked door, and ordered the rest to return to their rooms.

"Ahmed, coming out, all clear?" he called over the radio, and got a quick affirmative. The sniper had come up through the tunnel after them, to establish the first check point and take out the base sensors. In the darkness, the sniper's flashlight blinked on and off. Agostine flipped channels over to the pilot's channel, and called, "Shortbus, execute!", then turned back to the huddled prisoners.

"Roger, Lost Boys, two mikes, rotors hot. Shortbus on the way!" In the distance he heard the Osprey rev up, and turned back to the liberated prisoners.

"Everyone, run towards the flashlight, there are other soldiers who will guide you towards a landing zone. If any of you break away, you will be shot. MOVE!" he yelled at them, and they started running. Doc Hamilton took the second group and carefully encouraged them, helping two who were having a hard time moving.

"Team Two, under heavy fire" crackled the radio over the team net, *"falling back!"* Jones's voice sounded harsh, and even as he transmitted, there was the bang of Reynolds' rifle.

"See you at the RP! Six out," answered Agostine. He turned and went back into the building, in time to almost get shot by Zivcovic. Stepping in front the man's gun, placing himself between Singh, Zivcovic and the terrified scientists.

"I can't let you do this, Rachel. Regardless of what they've done, they're still human beings."

"Nick, get out of the way," she answered, not lowering her pistol.

He folded his arms resolutely and said, "No. I know what it's like to be in Invy captivity."

"And you resisted, even when they ate your leg," she said.

"I'm a trained soldier, we have no idea what or why they did what they did," he shot back.

She answered with a tortured, pleading look on her face, "Nick, I have MY orders, please move!"

From behind him, he heard a man yell, "They have our families!"

Agostine turned to answer the scientist, and Singh shot him in the leg, shattering the prosthetic. The Master Sergeant fell to the ground, off balance, and she started firing indiscriminately into the crowd with her rifle. They screamed and ran, ducking back towards rooms or towards the door.

"NO!" shouted Zivcovic and slapped the barrel down, hauling Agostine to his feet. "There is no honor in what you are doing, killing unarmed people!" said the Serb. He walked out the door, shaking his head.

"Jesus Christ, I can't believe you shot me," said Agostine, leaning against the wall, then he snapped, "LET GO OF ME!" as she reached for his arm. He had long ago learned to get around on one leg, and carried a collapsible cane strapped to his vest, just in case.

"You disgust me," he said harshly. "These are fucking human beings, and you don't know why they cooperated. You just want to shoot them out of hand to deny the Invy their talent. That makes you a damned murderer."

"How many have you killed?" she shot back. "Innocents!"

He shook his head, and said, "Not on purpose, and I never executed anyone except soldiers who fell asleep on duty, and they knew it when they joined up. And I still regret it."

"It was my orders," she said flatly.

"And some orders should be disobeyed, Rachel. That's what makes us better than them. Or what makes me better than them. You … I have nothing to say to you anymore."

Reaching down, he tore off the shattered prosthetic to the sound of ripping Velcro, surrounded by a pool of blood. Slinging his rifle across his chest, he started out the door in a lurching motion, leaving Singh behind, looking down at the wounded and dead scientists.

"Doc, gimme a SITREP, and do NOT let Singh anywhere near the POW's," called Agostine as soon as he got outside.

"Loading the bird now, got it. Busy," came back Hamilton.

"Nick, WAIT! I was only doing what I was ordered to do by CEF command!" called Singh, catching up to him. There was a pleading note in her voice.

He shrugged off her hand, and growled, "Touch me again, and I'll shoot you, I swear to God. We're done."

The NCO walked into the darkness, leaving Rachel Singh standing alone and forlorn in a combat zone.

Chapter 85

Agostine watched as the Osprey lifted, powered forward, and shifted into horizontal flight, followed by plasma rifle bolts that were too diffused, at this distance, to do anything, even if they hit.

Behind him, the Brookhaven campus burned brightly. One of the structures struck by a rocket, or maybe plasma fire, had been highly flammable, for whatever reason, and burned like a torch. At his side stood Hamilton, and Ahmed, while Zivcovic sat on a nearby tree. Between them stood Colonel Singh. The two pathfinders had taken off already, headed back to NYC. No one said anything for a long minute.

Finally Agostine spoke. "Ziv, I want you to escort Colonel Singh back to the RP. We're going to try and round up some of the other scientists and bring them back. Make sure nothing happens to her; she has a war to fight. " The sarcasm in the last sentence was marked.

"What about Reynolds?" asked the Serb.

"She's with us," he said.

"She is my partner," was his answer.

"I need her, just do what I told you."

Singh abruptly drew her pistol and pointed it at Agostine, and no one moved. She held it steady on him for a very long time, then holstered it. "We'll talk when we get back," the Colonel said, and walked into the darkness. Zivcovic shook his head and followed her.

"Let's go," said Agostine, and, without a backwards glance, lowered his face shield, got his bearings, and started hobbling westward. He needed to get back to the house where they had stashed their packs and strap on his extra carbon fiber blade prosthetic. The Scout was furious, and his heart was ash cold, feeling betrayed by Singh. Hell, they had fought together for years, and Singh had saved his life when he was an Invy prisoner.

"Nick," said Ahmed, coming up beside him, "you did the right thing,"

"I don't know, brother. In my head, I feel it was the smart thing to do, not leave any of them for the Invy to use for research. The strategic thing to do, even." His voice trailed off as he expressed his doubts.

"In the Quran, the Prophet tells us to listen to our hearts, and all else will follow. You know that Brittany would have stopped it, and she is your heart."

Agostine said, "Was my heart, Ahmed."

"Is, my brother. She is alive, somewhere, in another place, and you and she are together. I believe that there are many worlds where all things are possible," answered the older man.

Agostine laughed bitterly. "You mean someplace where we have some kids and a farm and a future?"

The sniper said, "Well, I would not go that far. I'm sure you would be involved in a fight somewhere, a noble one, like this one. It is what you are. But happy, yes."

They said nothing else until they reached the safe house. Agostine, with long practice, slipped the prosthetic out of his rolled up sleeping pad and strapped it onto his leg. He had just finished when a series of flashes lit the horizon, and muted booms from a shotgun firing echoed through the pines. His radio crackled to life, Singh's urgent voice calling, *"CONTACT! UNDER HEAVY FI-",* cutting off abruptly in mid-sentence.

"Shit!" he exclaimed. The other men dropped their packs and all three set out in a rush toward the sound of the gunfire. There was the hiss crack of plasma, followed by more shotgun blasts, and maybe the suppressed P-90, hard to tell through the trees. It stopped before they came close, and they advanced cautiously, scanning the area.

Suddenly the sound of blades clashing rang out, and they heard a loud yell, more steel clashing, and then silence. All thoughts of their disagreement forgotten, Agostine charged ahead, rifle up, Hamilton and Yassir beside him. They burst into a clearing just in time to see Zivcovic fall under a Dragon, his knife sticking out of the side of the creature's neck. There was another twitching on the ground at his feet. Four Wolverines stood motionless, and there were two dead on the ground. Each man fired, rules of honor be damned, instinctively choosing targets that matched their position. Two of the Invy went down, and, lighting quick, the other two moved, firing back.

Nick Agostine felt the plasma bolt hit him in the upper shoulder, but no pain as he fell to the ground. The shots and sounds died away, and he stared up at the stars, helmet knocked off his head. The grass felt cool in the October night, the ground firm beneath him, and time slowed, and then stopped.

"Nick!" said a voice, and he turned his head. It seemed as if it were daylight, and, sitting there on the ground beside him, barefoot and wearing a simple dress, was a redheaded woman with ice blue eyes.

"Are you going to lay there forever?" she laughed, and smiled. "There's corn to harvest, and you promised to take Jane fishing,"

"Brit?" he asked, reaching for her hand. It felt warm to his touch, smooth and alive.

"Of course. Come, we have a life to live. You did good, love." She stood and helped him up, and he took her in his arms, laughed, and carried her away towards the farm.

***

In the real world, Doc Hamilton screamed into the radio, "I DON"T FUCKING CARE! GET YOUR ASS BACK HERE!" Turning back to the still form of his friend, he frantically pumped nanos into Agostine's blood stream, spraying quick clot over the burned area. There was a no heartbeat, but his friend had a strange smile on his face.

"Don't you die on me!" yelled Hamilton. Singh put her hand on the medic's arm, but he shoved her away violently and kept working.

"Doc," said Ahmed, "tell me what to do."

"In my aide bag, there's a set of paddles. Sometimes a hit with a plasma bolt will overload a person's electrical charge, stopping the heart. Get them for me, quick."

Without any further words, the two men spent the next few minutes trying to bring back life to Nick Agostine, while his soul wandered through a beautiful, different reality. In the end, it was enough, just barely enough. A faint heartbeat appeared, and his vitals came back online in Doc's helmet display.

While they worked, Singh walked over to where Zivcovic lay under the Dragon's body, placed her hands under it, and heaved, rolling the stinking corpse off him. She first bent to check his pulse, but then stopped. The Serb had the Dragons' sword in his chest, and his knife was buried up to the hilt in the Invy's neck, their blood mixed together in a steaming pool on the sandy soil. He looked dead, until a slight movement of his eye lids showed. She checked his pulse, afraid to move the sword. It was there, barely. "DOC!" she started to shout, but the Serb reached up, gripped her arm and pulled her close.

"That... was a good fight. Tell that puss Agostine ... I will keep Brit company until he joins us. Maybe," he whispered, coughing up blood, "maybe she will love me instead, in next life..." He laughed, choking, until he fell still, a smile on his scarred face.

At that moment, Reynolds ran into the clearing, saw Zivcovic, and rushed over. She knelt by his body and cradled his head in her arms, weeping furiously. When Singh tried to comfort her, she screamed her grief at the other woman, making her back away.

Rachel Singh stood despondent in the clearing, surrounded by the dead, wounded and grieving, and wondered how it all could have gone so badly. Eventually, she started walking towards the rendezvous site, leaving the rest of the team behind.

The Osprey powered up its rotors, carrying a barely alive Nick Agostine away, and the team left the Serb surrounded by the bodies of his enemies. Reynolds placed his knife in his hand, piled the weapons of his victory around him, kissed his bloody face once, and placed an antimatter demo charge under his body. Ten minutes later, as they collected their packs, the horizon lit with brilliant fire, rivaling the heart of the sun.

Interlude

The sun rose again, as it always did, and General Dalpe fell asleep on a cot in the Operations Center. Major Padilla took a moment from coordinating movement of Main Force elements and Operational Detachments to ask an orderly to get a blanket.

The day had gone better than they had hoped; more than fifty percent of the attacks had been successful. They had gained control of major bases in the Pacific Northwest, California, Texas and the Northeast, though fighting was heavy in the New York City area, and Colorado was still in doubt. Consulting with the Naval Liaison, Rear Admiral Harris, Padilla asked that the Atlantic submarines move toward New York harbor to launch Tomahawk strikes. It technically wasn't his call, since Padilla was normally involved with the ODA's and only a Major, but Dalpe was exhausted.

"Cascade base reports their coms with ground units reestablished, SeaTac Airport secured," said a communications sergeant.

Colonel Jameson's face lit up, and he smiled broadly. "Let's get those fighters out of storage and in the air. I want a general recall of pilots from all recaptured towns ASAP, get the helos flying to pick them up." Between SeaTac, Andrews Air Force Base, and Travis in California, he had enough runway to take the fight to the enemy. They had the planes, he just needed the pilots. "I don't give a shit if the last thing they flew was a crop duster."

"Any word from Warren?" asked Padilla, looking at the ansible receiver.

"Nothing, Sir," said the commo sergeant. "Carrier wave is open, but he's plugged into the combat net, and not answering."

"Well," said Jameson, "now we wait. If he doesn't take out those cruisers, we're toast."

"Agreed," said Padilla, pulling a deck of cards from his pocket. "Admiral, do you play spades, by any chance?"

"I'm a sailor, son. We're born with cards in our hands," said the older man. He reached out, took the deck, and started to shuffle. "Dollars a point, Joker, joker, deuce, deuce, ace. I'll take Colonel Jameson as my partner."

"Sergeant Robles," smiled Padilla, "it looks like he does know how to play. Let's show these old men how it's done!"

As Admiral Harris handed out the cards, over their heads, a million miles away, the spaceships danced in a complicated, many pointed geometry of death; and on Earth, men and women died, fighting to be free.

To be continued in Invasion Book 3: Total War…

If you enjoyed this book, please check out my other titles, including the award winning Irregular Scout Team One post-apocalyptic series.

https://amazon.com/author/johnholmes

Follow me on Amazon, send me a friend request on Facebook, and join the Irregular Scouts!

My books:

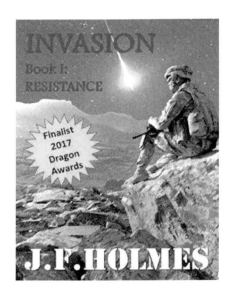

Invasion:

1. Resistance*

2. Day of Battle (on Sale Nov 15th)

3. War (2018)

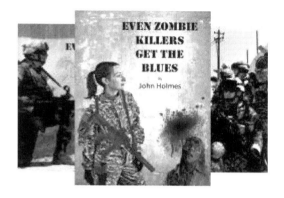

The Irregular Scout Team Series:

1. Even Zombie Killers Get The Blues
2. Even Zombie Killers Need a Break
3. Even Zombie Killers Can Die
4. ZK: Civil War
5. ZK: Endgame
6. ZK: Ambush
7. ZK: Heat
8. ZK: Bad Company
0. ZK: Falling (Prequel) *
9: ZK: Scouts Out (2018)

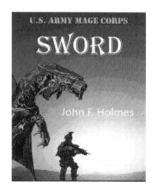

Mage Corps Series:

Sword
Nightfall (2018)

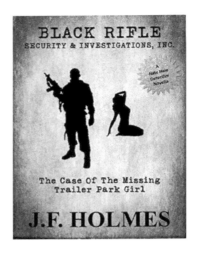

Black Rifle Security & Investigations Novellas:

The Case of the Missing Trailer Park Girl
The Case of the Gangsters Daughter
The Case of the Lucky Cat (2018)

Non-series books:

Under A Different Sun (Space Opera)
Direct Action: Cyber (Technothriller)
Princess Wilma & The Pirate King (YA Fantasy)
Sea Of Fire (Fantasy)
There and Back Again, a Fobbit's Journey.

* Dragon Award Nominees

Printed in Great Britain
by Amazon